BARE HUNT

*The Serial Killer Is Back
And Hunting His Prey*

———∞———

S.M. Sedgwick

Copyright © S.M. Sedgwick 2022
This book is sold subject to the condition that it shall not, by way of trade or otherwise, be lent, resold, hired out, or otherwise circulated without the publisher's prior consent in any form of binding or cover other than that in which it is published and without a similar condition including this condition being imposed on the subsequent publisher.
The moral right of S.M. Sedgwick has been asserted.
ISBN-13:

This is a work of fiction. Names, characters, businesses, organisations, places, events and incidents either are the product of the author's imagination or are used fictitiously. Any resemblance to actual persons, living or dead, events, or locales is entirely coincidental.

For the grandchildren.
You can be anything you want to be in this world,
but most importantly, be kind.

"The basic test of a police force is that it should arrest more criminals than it employs."
Sir Robert Mark, Metropolitan Police Commissioner 1972-77

Thanks to all those that have contributed,

some knowingly, some unknowingly.

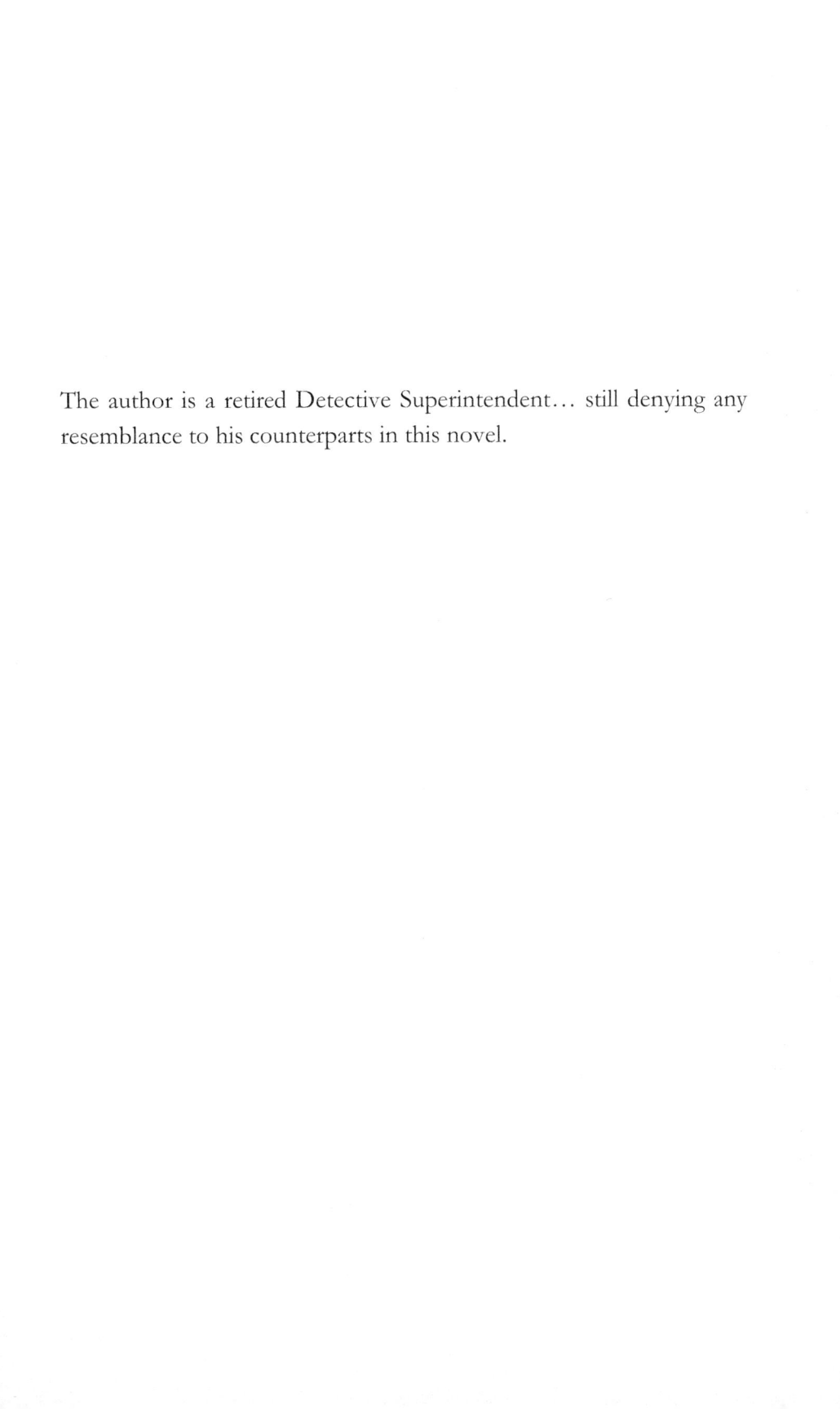

The author is a retired Detective Superintendent… still denying any resemblance to his counterparts in this novel.

CONTENTS

PROLOGUE 1
CHAPTER 1 3
CHAPTER 2 6
CHAPTER 3 9
CHAPTER 4 13
CHAPTER 5 16
CHAPTER 6 19
CHAPTER 7 23
CHAPTER 8 26
CHAPTER 9 29
CHAPTER 10 33
CHAPTER 11 35
CHAPTER 12 38
CHAPTER 13 40
CHAPTER 14 43
CHAPTER 15 47
CHAPTER 16 50
CHAPTER 17 53
CHAPTER 18 55
CHAPTER 19 57
CHAPTER 20 60
CHAPTER 21 63
CHAPTER 22 66
CHAPTER 23 69
CHAPTER 24 72
CHAPTER 25 76
CHAPTER 26 78
CHAPTER 27 80
CHAPTER 28 84
CHAPTER 29 87
CHAPTER 30 90
CHAPTER 31 93
CHAPTER 32 95
CHAPTER 33 97

CHAPTER 34	100
CHAPTER 35	103
CHAPTER 36	106
CHAPTER 37	108
CHAPTER 38	110
CHAPTER 39	113
CHAPTER 40	116
CHAPTER 41	119
CHAPTER 42	123
CHAPTER 43	126
CHAPTER 44	129
CHAPTER 45	131
CHAPTER 46	133
CHAPTER 47	136
CHAPTER 48	139
CHAPTER 49	142
CHAPTER 50	144
CHAPTER 51	147
CHAPTER 52	150
CHAPTER 53	152
CHAPTER 54	155
CHAPTER 55	158
CHAPTER 56	161
CHAPTER 57	164
CHAPTER 58	166
CHAPTER 59	168
CHAPTER 60	171
CHAPTER 61	173
CHAPTER 62	176
CHAPTER 63	179
CHAPTER 64	182
CHAPTER 65	185
CHAPTER 66	188
CHAPTER 67	191
CHAPTER 68	194
CHAPTER 69	197
CHAPTER 70	200

CHAPTER 71	203
CHAPTER 72	206
CHAPTER 73	209
CHAPTER 74	212
CHAPTER 75	215
CHAPTER 76	218
CHAPTER 77	221
CHAPTER 78	224
CHAPTER 79	227
CHAPTER 80	230
CHAPTER 81	235
EPILOGUE	239

PROLOGUE

He had not killed anyone for nearly a year and considered this to be validation of the fact that he was once more back in control of his own actions and desires. The unwanted public attention surrounding his previous exploits had subsided with the focus on the new serial killer in town: the global pandemic was even more indiscriminate than he had ever been and had left a trail of victims in its wake. It did mean, however, that as he stepped outside, his disguised appearance was aided and abetted by a face mask, providing him with even more confidence that there would be no recognition of his former self.

The world felt different as people around him proceeded with less certainty in their actions which contrasted his own resolution and determination. Patience had been a necessity but as time progressed it was becoming less of a restraint. As he paused to look into a shop window his peripheral vision picked up the sight of two uniformed police officers walking toward him. Nothing in their demeanour suggested any great purpose but he instinctively took hold of his companion's hand, knowing that a middle-aged couple were somehow more invisible than a solitary pedestrian.

She was pleased with the unexpected display of apparent affection but tried to be nonchalant in the hope it would last longer. However, after the police officers had passed he immediately released his hold and the hand fell reluctantly to her side. His attention returned to the window display of camping supplies and fishing tackle.

"You should be able to get them in here," he asserted and she replied with an obedient silent nod before entering the store alone. Even with a shaven head and face mask on he had no wish to feature on any in-store CCTV systems. Whilst waiting he browsed the internet on his phone, allowing him to keep his head bowed and avoid eye contact with passing strangers. The chance of recognition was incredibly slim but it remained a risk and the new version of Paul Avery was intent on eliminating as many risks as possible, particularly during the preparatory stages of his plan.

She returned after a few minutes and the new bag she was carrying suggested a purchase had been made. Initially she began to hold it open to allow his inspection of the contents but his angry glare told her this was neither the time nor place. She mumbled an apology that was not acknowledged and the pair walked back toward their vehicle parked nearby.

Only when the small town was in her rear-view mirror did the passenger open the bag to view the pair of leather-sheafed hunting knives. His smile suggested she had selected well and she breathed an inward sigh of relief as he instructed her to drive home. Confident that his attention was elsewhere she stole an occasional glance in his direction and wished she could do more to please him. Then she remembered his promise that one day he would need her more than he had needed anyone before and her heart soared.

CHAPTER 1

Twenty-Three Years Ago

The interview had gone well and Avery was confident that he would be offered the opportunity to pursue a career in the police service. He replayed some of the questions and answers in his mind as he drove home, allowing himself to daydream about putting on the uniform for the first time with all the opportunities that would afford. That lack of concentration for the relatively inexperienced driver caused him to take a last-second evasive manoeuvre in order to avoid the cyclist he had failed to spot on the quiet country road.

It would have remained a near miss without repercussion had the cyclist not reacted with such an angry retaliatory gesture directed toward Avery as he was driving away. Indeed for a few seconds Avery was going to ignore it until the indignation of being abused for such a minor occurrence overwhelmed him.

A lay-by approximately a mile further along the road gave him the opportunity to park and wait for the cyclist to catch him up and he calculated that with the incline of the road working against the cyclist, he would have a couple of minutes to formulate a plan. Sure enough, after a short time he saw his target in the offside door mirror and he allowed the young man to overtake his stationary vehicle.

Michael Warner was an introverted and meek man who having spotted the parked vehicle ahead of him, regretted his uncharacteristic angry gesture that the earlier near miss had provoked. He therefore fixed his gaze straight ahead as he cycled past the car in the vain hope that would be the end of the matter. The sound of the car emerging from the lay-by behind him caused him some disquiet, especially as the hilly coastal road prevented him from picking up any great speed.

He was aware that the car was driving slowly behind him even though the road was quite narrow in parts and there was ample room to overtake. He guessed that the intention was to intimidate him and wondered if the car driver realised how effective the tactic was. He knew the road well and looked forward to the next turn which would lead to the crest of the hill followed by a long downhill straight. At the bottom of the straight was the opportunity to divert onto a small track that he often used as a route home but which was thankfully inaccessible to cars.

Avery also knew the road well having grown up in the local area and was also waiting for the same stretch of road. As the pair rounded the bend in convoy, the gap between car and cycle grew larger as Avery temporarily braked. Once he was satisfied there were no oncoming vehicles he accelerated by pressing his right foot to the floor. Warner heard the increased engine noise behind him and assumed he was about to be overtaken in a similar fashion to the original encounter. Instead the impact of the car onto the rear of his bike sent him hurtling in the air until he made unwelcome contact with the unforgiving tarmac.

As he lay on the road he knew he was injured but was reluctant to move in case this made the pain worse. This inaction eliminated any possibility of avoiding his assailant's car, which was now reversing at full speed toward him.

In total Avery ran over the prone body four times before he was satisfied enough to stop the car and emerge. Although the road was usually incredibly quiet he wasted no time in putting the cyclist's body in the boot of his car before hiding the damaged cycle in some nearby undergrowth. He made a mental note of its precise location so he could recover it later. He was thankful that despite the horrific injuries he had caused there was relatively little blood on the road. Nevertheless, he disguised its presence with a combination of roadside mud and sand before returning to his car. A cursory check of the damage to his vehicle showed it pleasingly to be superficial and something he was confident of correcting without the need for third-party assistance.

By the following morning he had disposed of both body and cycle by burying them in different locations. He had also studied the contents of Michael Warner's wallet and small rucksack to gain a retrospective insight into the life of his victim. Such was the wealth of material available to him it was with some confidence that he knocked on the door at Warner's home address at 3pm the following day.

The door was opened by a woman in her late 50s who Avery correctly assumed to be the mother of his victim.

"Sorry to disturb you, Mrs Warner, I was just wondering if Michael was at home?" enquired Avery with a smile he hoped would be reassuring .

"No, I'm afraid he isn't, he didn't come home last night. I don't know where he is actually and I'm very worried," said Linda Warner. And then as an apologetic afterthought, "I'm sorry, who are you?"

"My name is Michael too. I'm a friend of your Michael and wondered if I might have a chat with you."

"Yes, of course, Michael didn't tell me he had a friend. Please come in," she replied, anxious to receive any news about her son.

CHAPTER 2

It didn't take long for Avery to build an accurate pen picture of his victim and the rather pitiful existence he shared with this woman. She seemingly had an unabated desire to share the intimate details of her life with a man who had entered her home as a stranger minutes beforehand. He had concocted an elaborate cover story but had barely needed to use it as Mrs Warner rarely paused for breath.

The worried mother was instead relieved that the burden of her son's uncharacteristic disappearance was being shared by his friend and happily allowed access to his room so Avery could look for any clues that might explain it. Rather than accompany him she busied herself making the coffee that Avery had subliminally suggested, whilst apologising for her lack of hospitality.

The bedroom was that of a stereotypical loner and the array of computer games suggested Michael Warner had spent hours of gaming solitude as an alternative to the experiences of real life. Avery quietly opened and closed drawers and cupboards in the room, pausing briefly to gaze at their uninteresting contents. He was both surprised and delighted to discover that Michael kept a written diary and made a cursory examination of it before slipping it nonchalantly into his jacket pocket. At that moment Mrs Warner entered the room carrying his mug of coffee.

"Do you think I should call the police, Michael?" she asked before immediately voicing her own self-doubt. "I mean it hasn't even been twenty-four hours but it's so unlike him."

"Well of course you could, but I don't think it's the right thing to do. You see Michael told me the other day that he was thinking of going away for a few days because he needed some space. I know where he might have gone. Are you happy to let me find him rather than make the situation worse by involving the police?"

Whilst not fully understanding her son's need for 'space' she could not have been more happy to entrust his friend with the task he had so kindly volunteered to undertake, and gave him a tearful hug of appreciation. Avery struggled not to spill his coffee such was the intensity of the embrace but managed to utter some soothing platitudes to reinforce his position as the saviour of the situation.

The pair returned to the lounge whereupon Avery expanded on his friendship with Michael and how the young men had bonded over a mutual love of computer games. He was astute enough to read her nonverbal communication well enough to give an illusion of knowing her son well and they laughed at some of his mannerisms. He learned that mother and son had no other immediate family following the death of her husband some years earlier and it appeared that her sole role in life was to care for her only child even though he was now an adult. Avery made a series of mental notes and struggled to contain his amusement that the random victim was offering him so many future opportunities.

After three hours of his invested time Avery called a halt to the meeting and promised to return the following day with an update regarding the whereabouts of Michael Warner. He received another warm, almost maternal embrace of gratitude before leaving and used the drive home to formulate a detailed plan in his mind.

True to his word he returned the following day, and every day for a week thereafter, gradually building the trust and manipulating the situation in a perfectly contrived manner. A few days after a day trip to France (which had allowed Avery to stock up on some rather nice red wine), he again visited her and was unsurprised to find a very happy Mrs Warner.

"Michael, look what came yesterday, he's in Paris!" she exclaimed before thrusting the postcard into Avery's hand.

Avery did his best to portray a bemused expression as he read the postcard he had authored earlier that week. He read it aloud and hesitated whilst appearing to struggle to interpret the words on the card. This caused her to laugh and retrieve the communication whilst rebuking her absent son about the state of his handwriting. This confirmed to Avery that the fraudulent prose he had constructed had been accepted as authentic by its recipient.

"Mum, I hope I haven't worried you too much but I needed to get away and sort my life out. Things have not been right for a while and I just needed a fresh start. Once I am settled I will be in touch, love M," she read, but in truth she did not need to as she had memorised the words after repeatedly scanning the card. She then held the card close to her chest as though it were an embrace of her missing son.

"It's good news, isn't it, Michael? It shows he's okay?"

He smiled and nodded a silent affirmation to the rhetorical question before replacing her virtual hug with a real one. Avery didn't believe in fate but he had to concede that his brief interaction with Michael Warner had been the closest he had ever come to accepting its existence.

CHAPTER 3

Present Day

Bare sat outside his new boss's office like an errant schoolboy summoned to see the headteacher. The preceding months had been a blur of recuperating whilst on sick leave, owed annual leave he had been required to take and then 'assisting' the formal enquiry that followed in the wake of everything that had preceded it. All of these had delayed the inevitable meeting that would determine his future.

The 'formal review' of everything connected to Avery had been conducted by the Constabulary in conjunction with the Independent Office for Police Conduct (IOPC). There had been considerable tension between the two organisations, as each would have preferred sole jurisdiction but Avery's 'missing presumed dead' status blurred the lines for both. The Constabulary were happy that his death drew a line under the complex and intertwined investigations but were equally adept at using the lack of absolute certainty as to his demise when it suited. The IOPC knew they were limited when an 'active' murder investigation was being conducted and correctly sensed there were political forces active in order to minimise the collateral damage to reputations and careers. The net result was an uneasy compromise with outcomes that satisfied neither party.

In truth this particular serial killer had not particularly whetted the public appetite, which had readily accepted the explanation that this was a 'psychotic episode of an otherwise excellent cop'.

Bare cynically observed that, as the known victims were almost exclusively members of the police service or criminals, this lacked a true independent heroic victim necessary for public outrage. He held begrudging respect for the manner in which the Constabulary had managed the media to the extent that he barely recognised the story to which he had been so central. Of course a global pandemic had assisted the process; if ever there was a time to bury bad news it had to be when the collective eyes of the world were so firmly facing the other direction.

Bare now sensed that he was perceived as an inconvenient 'loose end' and wondered how the imminent meeting would seek to address that. He had recognised during the review that the Constabulary were uncertain as to how to treat him. On the one hand he was the grieving widower who had literally taken a bullet to save an innocent child. This was very good press and much needed to deflect the actions of Avery. On the other hand there had been deep suspicions about his culpability and relationships with the McKenzie Organised Crime Group, making it necessary to limit the scope of the review for fear of turning the whole thing into some 'awful tacky soap opera', which had been the term used by the Chief Constable.

*

Any further contemplation was interrupted by the sight of Detective Superintendent Sarah Woodham appearing from her office and walking toward him with an outstretched arm.

"Sebastian, it's so good to see you looking so well. Please come in."

He dutifully shook her hand and followed her into the office whilst covertly signalling Ann, the PA, that he would welcome a coffee. Ann's winked response put him a little more at ease until he walked into the office with all the associated memories of its former occupant. The present incumbent motioned for him to take a seat on the newly installed formal-looking sofa and surprisingly sat alongside him. Bare was suspicious of this approach, preferring the traditional seats separated by an austere desk favoured by 'old school' superintendents. He had only briefly met Woodham once before but her reputation preceded her. She was the antipathy of 'old school', a modern-thinking and politically astute high flier wrapped up in a very personable exterior. The Corporate Communications staff loved her and she had been used as the 'talking head' of the Constabulary frequently, with her calm authoritative tone presenting exactly the right image for a progressive organisation.

"Shall we cut to the chase, Sebastian? I've been speaking with the Chief and we wonder if you have considered a medical retirement."

"Is that a question or a suggestion, ma'am?" replied Bare, quickly realising how the Constabulary were viewing this particular 'loose end'.

"There would be a generous settlement and immediate access to a full pension. Given everything you have been through I think it would be worth considering, Sebastian," she said with a smile designed to encourage acquiescence.

Bare's reply was stopped by a knock on the door and Ann's entry carrying a small tray with two coffees on it.

"Oh, Ann, how thoughtful," said Woodham, annoyed at the uninvited interruption.

There was an uneasy silence in the room as the cups were transferred from tray to small coffee table and the few seconds allowed Bare to formulate a better answer in his mind. After Ann had departed he vocalised his rephrased response.

"What if I don't wish to take premature retirement?" he asked.

"Then of course we would be delighted that a man with your vast experience would be remaining in the Service, we would just need to find you a suitable position," she answered, quickly signifying this was the expected course of the conversation.

"And I am guessing my present role would not be considered suitable?"

"Well you don't really have a present role, do you Sebastian, having been away for several months. Your previous role has now been permanently assigned to Sharon Brady and I think you will agree we were lucky to get her."

Bare smiled at the mention of the one officer he would never object to replacing him and sensed he was about to learn of his own proposed 'punishment posting'. However, it was time for him to play his own cards rather than passively accept his fate.

"I want to be promoted, I want a DI's job and if I am unsuccessful I will retire as suggested and use the time to pursue other career avenues," he said, whilst handing Woodham a letter from an inner pocket of his suit jacket.

Bare took a sip of the hot coffee whilst Woodham quickly read the correspondence from the production company inviting Bare to have a starring role in the proposed documentary he had contacted them about. After digesting the contents of the letter Woodham politely returned it to him.

"I'll speak to the Chief. Take care of yourself, Sebastian," she said, signalling that the meeting was at an end.

CHAPTER 4

Avery lay in his bed reminiscing about how he had killed the original Michael Warner all those years ago. All the subsequent investment of his time in creating a duplicate identity just in case he had the need for a safety net had been worthwhile, because the one thing you really need when falling from a high cliff is a robust safety net. His surrogate mother could not have been better suited, a woman of limited intelligence whose sole purpose in life had been to look after her equally stupid son. The original Michael Warner was probably now more alive in Avery's mind than his mother's as the former replayed the images of his brutal demise.

For a few months she had believed he was living abroad and had been content – no, happy – to give up his bed to Avery who had told her that he had become estranged from his own mother. Once Avery had moved in the communications from her son had become more sporadic and their content increasingly spiteful toward her, to the extent she had stopped reading them. Instead she passed them to Avery without suspicion that she was in fact returning the literature to its author.

She had, unsurprisingly, cried upon learning of Michael's death in France but by then she had adopted a better version and was thrilled when Michael 2.0 asked if he could formally change his surname to Warner to reinforce his love for the mother he never had. Thereafter, correspondence addressed to Michael Warner regularly arrived at the family home and it was always dutifully placed to one side to await Michael's attention when his very important job allowed him to return home. And of course, Michael always came home for Christmas.

Last Christmas had of course been different; he had not arrived with his normal exuberant swagger weighed down with armfuls of extravagant presents. Instead he had been like a wounded pet using only instinct and determination to get home, but somehow she loved him even more because of that. She had tended his wounds without question as to their origin and had once again become the mother she was born to be. The arrival of her carer on Boxing Day had wrong-footed him, as this was a new development in her life that he had been unprepared for. He had beaten a hasty retreat to his room and listened intently through the door to his mother's explanation about the arrival of her son from abroad who had taken to his bed unwell. The concept of self-isolation was beginning to be readily accepted so whilst he heard the carer express some concern, it had been mainly for the welfare of her customer.

He had waited a full fortnight before briefly introducing himself to her. By then his shaven head and facial hair made him look completely different from any photographs that were still circulating in the media. A pair of glasses added to the disguise, an astute mail-order purchase that had arrived the day before. Were he not covertly studying her every move he would have struggled to remember her as she was the personification of a nondescript 40-year-old woman.

"Pleased to meet you, Sonia. I've heard so much about you from my mum."

"Nice to meet you too. I hope you're feeling better now?" she had replied with the accompaniment of a weak handshake.

He had kept their interactions to a minimum for the first few weeks, gradually assessing Sonia in order to determine the level of risk she presented. It emerged that she was the daughter of a former neighbour of the Warners but thankfully they had only moved in post Michael Version One's demise. She was single with no children and had given up her previous employment as a cashier at the local supermarket to provide live-in care to her terminally ill mother. During this time she had become acquainted with the increasingly fragile Mrs Warner so following the death of her own mother had offered to provide occasional care for her. This had increased and been refined over the last few months to the extent that she came in most days for a few hours to assist with general domestic issues. Avery had barely recognised the deterioration in Linda Warner's health until he realised how dependent she was becoming on her 'guardian angel' Sonia.

Although he felt no empathy he understood that the pair had probably developed a symbiotic relationship with the care being provided in exchange for the void caused by a recent bereavement. His 'return home' obviously presented an opportunity to dispense with the services of Sonia which would have eliminated all risks to himself but the trade-off for this was actually undertaking some care issues himself, which frankly was an abhorrent consideration. Besides, it was useful having a daily litmus test as to what was happening in the outside world without having to leave the sanctuary of his house.

As the weeks passed he had noticed that Sonia's initial shyness toward him was dissipating. She seemed to be making more effort with her appearance and dress, even clumsily attempting a flirtatious remark on one occasion, resulting in her reddening at her own audacity. For his part Avery was content for this to progress. The more relaxed she was in his company the more his influence over her would grow. He had learned salutary lessons from the preceding twelve months and perhaps the biggest was that patience and planning could not give way to desire.

CHAPTER 5

Promotion Boards were a lot easier when you knew the questions in advance, Bare concluded as he left the panel to consider his performance. He decided to call into his old office and was pleased to see his replacement sitting alone pensively studying the crime report on her desk.

"Another work of fiction designed to hike up the detection rate?" he ventured as he walked into the room.

"Well hello, stranger. How did it go?" she asked in a tone that suggested she was genuinely pleased to see him.

"You can never tell but hopefully they will feel sorry for me this time," he replied.

"Oh, Mr Modest really doesn't suit you, I'm sure you won them over with all that fraudulent charm, especially Ms Woodham," teased Brady.

"I'm not sure she likes me but then I can never guess what a woman is thinking," he countered.

"Well, you had better get promoted, Sebastian, as you can't have your job back," she laughed whilst protectively grabbing a full in-tray of documents. "I mean, who would want to lose all this excitement!"

Bare ignored the sarcasm and offered to buy her a coffee and she readily accepted the proposal. The sparsely populated canteen allowed them to sit at their table of choice and gradually the tension that had been present during their previous brief meetings started to erode. Brady still retained some frustration that the events of the previous year had not been fully shared by Bare and she had come to realise the pair would never recover the full intimacy of their previous relationship. Nevertheless, she took her position as unofficial counsellor to maverick police officers very seriously so resumed her probing after her first sip of the hot latte he had bought her.

"So has the paranoia eased, Mr Bare?" she asked mischievously.

"If you're asking whether I have fully accepted his apparent demise, then the answer remains no," he replied after checking the proximity of any potential eavesdroppers so often found in police canteens.

"A thousand to one he survived the fall and then another thousand to one he managed to remain undiscovered," reminded Brady.

"Yet I guarantee someone will win the lottery this weekend at much greater odds," countered Bare. "But I accept that as each night passes I sleep a little easier," he lied in the hope that she would move onto another topic.

She didn't.

"But no more sightings?"

Bare flinched as the simple question still evoked the memory of the day four months earlier when he had caused mayhem in the town centre by abandoning his car and rugby tackling an innocent pedestrian who bore a passing resemblance to Avery.

"No, no more sightings," he replied flatly. In truth there had been an average of at least one a day to accompany the vivid imagery of the nightmares that interrupted his sleep.

"Okay, no more therapy," said Brady, raising her palm as a gesture of defeat. "How's Robin?"

Bare took a sip of his coffee to delay answering and was now seriously doubting the wisdom of the meeting that he had instigated. Whilst he and Sharon Brady were now strictly platonic there was still something uncomfortable about being quizzed on a new relationship by an ex-girlfriend.

"She's fine, up to her eyes in work in London so not really spoken to her for a few days."

Brady knew him well enough to recognise that the dismissive tone of his voice signalled he didn't wish to elaborate and part of her was glad, as for some reason the thought of Bare with someone else still irked her much more than it should have.

They both took another strategic gulp of their beverages in the mutual hope that the encounter would not become awkward again, when his mobile phone came to life and became a welcome saviour. He answered it and was surprised to learn he was being summoned back to see his boss.

"Got to go, Ma'am wants a word," he said apologetically, rising to his feet.

"Must mean the promotion jury is back. Good luck," she offered, crossing fingers on both hands to emphasise the wish.

"Thanks. I'll let you know," he said as he quickly left to learn his fate.

Brady chose to remain in the canteen alone rather than return to her office and used the time to remonstrate with herself for caring so much about such a lost cause. She reminded herself that it really was time to move on.

CHAPTER 6

Avery closed the book having consumed its content in one lengthy sitting. It was, as far as he was aware, the only publication to date that sought to tell the story of the 'deranged senior police officer' who had murdered at least five people and attempted to kill three others including a child. He looked at the black and white photograph of its author, Amelia Hann, on the inside rear cover and tried to recall whether he had met her when she had been a journalist for the local rag. Her face was unfamiliar and he wondered whether she was a member of the Sebastian Bare Appreciation Society given the glowing terms in which his 'heroics' were described. It was a superficial and largely inaccurate read designed to cash in on the notoriety of 'Britain's most evil cop' as she had labelled him in chapter one, he concluded.

He dismissively dropped the book into the wicker waste bin in his room before retrieving it to avoid Sonia rescuing it when she cleaned later. The speed of its publication meant there were only a few photographs in the middle pages of the book and those were the same as had been run in the press in the immediate aftermath. The notable exception was the additional photograph of Julia Bare that he had never seen before, which he assumed had been supplied by Sebastian as it was clearly taken on a holiday. He reopened the book to look again at the smiling Julia sitting in some sun-drenched resort cheerfully toasting the photographer with a half-consumed glass of wine, and was instantly transported back to her bedroom when she lay naked on the bed before him.

He then turned to his own photograph and wondered why they had chosen that particular one, given it was several years old. He concluded it was because it showed him resplendent in full ceremonial police uniform to highlight the contrast between the image of good versus the reality of evil. After studying it closely he gazed into the wall mirror in his room and was reassured that his reflection now was only vaguely similar.

After secreting the book in plain sight amongst others on a crowded bookshelf he turned on the computer and waited patiently for it to load and obey his typed search instruction. There was a myriad of information about Amelia Hann including the fact that she was director of a small production company. Perhaps this signalled that the book was a mere precursor to some low-budget salacious television production, he mused, before concentrating his search on the Companies House website. From there, within a few clicks he had her date of birth and the correspondence address for the production company. He then researched this address to find out it was a residential property in a small village approximately thirty miles away. A few more clicks showed the estate agent's brochure that had been available at the time of the property sale two years ago. The house had a distinctive front porch and Avery didn't even need to retrieve the book to confirm Hann's publicity photo had been taken in front of her own house. It had taken him approximately five minutes to identify where she lived.

The knock on his door was his cue to close the windows on his browser before acknowledging the request to enter. As Sonia came into the room he glanced at his watch and noted she was thirty minutes early for work.

"You're keen today, Sonia," was his greeting and she smiled before providing some explanation that he had no interest in.

"Mrs Warner is asleep downstairs so is it okay if I clean in here first?" she asked, her voice failing to hide the nervous excitement she felt when alone with him.

"Yes, of course, I won't get in your way. I was just going for a shower anyway," he replied before rising from his chair and passing her in the narrow bedroom doorway. He touched her arm for an unnecessarily long time as he left the room and she felt her heartbeat accelerate at the action. After he had gone she checked herself in the same mirror he had used minutes earlier and hoped he liked her top that she had chosen to accentuate her breasts, the only physical feature she was remotely happy with. She allowed herself the briefest of smiles before recognising the reality of her reflection. She considered herself unremarkable and unworthy of a good-looking man's attention. Such was her low self-esteem she thought it foolish to hope otherwise and gave a short sigh.

She then busied herself with some superficial cleaning in the room that Michael always seemed to keep immaculate, not knowing why her duties had recently been extended to include this task. The noise of the shower in the bathroom ceased and she knew she ought to vacate his room but delayed her work a little longer in the hope it would lead to some more time in his company. After the briefest of intervals he appeared at the door, only partially dry and with a towel wrapped around his waist.

"Sorry, am just finishing," she said, dusting the same bedside table she had done earlier and averting her gaze from the direction where she desperately wanted to stare. He made no comment but she felt him standing behind her and she heard the towel drop to the floor. His arms encircled her waist and she felt his hot breath caress her neck moments before she felt the kiss that immediately followed.

She was so unfamiliar with this situation and wondered if she ought to make a token protest although she sensed he would be uncaring if she did. Instead she allowed her hand to reach behind where she found him already hard and clearly very determined. Some items of her clothing were removed, others roughly pulled to one side before the act she had hoped would last for hours was over. There was no aftercare, no sweet platitudes and she was left to dress in silence as he lay on the bed watching her. She felt more alive than ever before. The silence ended as his mother called upstairs asking if she was there and she quickly left his room without looking back.

As he watched her go Avery was confident that the months of grooming had been completed with precision. She now belonged to him and would be a useful addition to his growing armoury.

CHAPTER 7

"It's customary to be pleased with a promotion, particularly when it's to the Detective Inspector role that you wanted," said Woodham with mock surprise at his reaction to the news.

"The Compliance and Intelligence Bureau is a desk job," said Bare, realising the Constabulary had acquiesced to his demands but at the same time exploited an opportunity to restrain and monitor his policing style.

"Well, most Inspector roles come with a desk these days and I'm sure there will be opportunities in the years ahead to explore other positions. So congratulations, Sebastian," was the smiling response delivered with corporate aplomb.

Bare had played the game long enough to know that any further comment would be futile so he acknowledged the manoeuvre and left her office.

"Congratulations, DI Bare, you can afford to buy me dinner now," said Ann as he walked past her, partly in jest.

"Oh come on, Ann, you know I would rather cook for you, be so much more intimate," was the reply with a cheeky wink.

"In your dreams, lover boy," she retorted without even looking up from her desk, reinforcing the fact that a good PA could easily flirt and work simultaneously.

After finding her office still empty Bare located Brady where he had left her in the canteen. His attempt at presenting a 'bad news' face had no effect whatsoever as she immediately rose to give him a prolonged congratulatory hug.

"But know this, Sebastian, I am never ever calling you 'sir'," she whispered in his ear.

"Well in that case I'm going to turn it down cause that's the only reason I put in for it," he replied, causing the pair to laugh together for the first time in a long time.

"They've stuck me in CIB," he added pre-empting her inevitable next question.

"Haha, sounds like the new management team have got you sussed already then," she teased, but she was secretly relieved he had been assigned a 'safe' position.

"Yeah, maybe. Besides, it's quite an important strategic role."

"Oh my god, they have activated the management chip already!" squealed Brady, unable to contain her shock, and again, the pair laughed in unison.

Bare's phone once again interrupted them and Brady took the opportunity to return to her office. She hoped that his promotion signified the start of a new chapter in his life and that the stability of the CIB position would improve the mental health of her friend. Despite all his bluster and denials she knew that the previous year's events were still at the forefront of his mind and that genuinely saddened her. As she walked toward her ever growing in-tray of crime reports she saw Sarah Woodham approach from the other direction. The pair's interaction had been limited but Woodham impressively greeted her by her first name.

"Hello, Sharon, how are you?" asked her boss and unlike the majority of her male predecessors waited for a response.

"Good thanks, ma'am," replied Brady, expecting that to be the end of the interaction.

"Excellent. I wonder if you might spare me a couple of minutes," said Woodham, motioning Brady to enter her own office. Woodham followed her in and closed the door behind her, the unsaid signal that she wanted the chat to be a confidential one.

"You've no doubt heard that we have decided to promote Sebastian Bare?" came the somewhat rhetorical question.

"Yes ma'am, excellent news," said Brady, unsure as to the direction of travel of the conversation.

"Yes, it's certainly good news for him," was the senior officer's oblique response before an immediate further question for Brady. "I'm told you're a good friend of his, is that correct?"

Brady felt herself reddening at the unexpected inquisition before confirming that was indeed the case.

"That's good to hear. I have heard good things about you, Sharon, and, to be honest, I was a little disappointed you didn't put in for the promotion boards yourself. Please don't allow your friendship with Mr Bare to jeopardise your future career prospects."

"Erm, I'm not entirely sure what you mean, ma'am," came the honest response.

Woodham smiled before expanding on her previous statement.

"Let's just say, under my watch the personnel at this station will live or die by adherence to policy and procedures. No shortcuts, no off-road adventures. My sense is there is still some institutionalised bullshit macho culture in this building, am I right?"

"I think there is considerably less than there used to be, ma'am," said Brady diplomatically.

"Well then we're heading in the right direction and I'm sure I can rely on you to guide others where necessary," said Woodham.

"Absolutely, ma'am," replied Brady, still trying to interpret the subtext of her senior officer.

CHAPTER 8

She was enjoying the rare silent intimacy as they lay in bed together before reluctantly breaking the spell with her words.

"I feel I've known you forever," she whispered.

Avery gave her an unusually affectionate kiss on her forehead to acknowledge he had heard the comment but made no verbal response. Undeterred, Sonia pressed on, knowing she had limited time before Mrs Warner would awake downstairs and be expecting a meal.

"I hope you won't be disappearing again anytime soon," Sonia continued. She had tried to keep her tone light hearted but he immediately recognised the genuine concern in her voice.

"I have some business to attend to but after that I think my future will involve a permanent move abroad," he replied and smiled as he heard her audible sigh of disappointment.

"Your mother is hoping you're back home for good," she replied, hoping that her own disappointment was disguised in her empathy for Mrs Warner.

She sat up and began slowly dressing when he leaned forward and whispered in her ear.

"Would you like to come with me and live a new life in the sun?"

"I would love that, but I think you're just teasing me," she replied whilst fervently hoping he wasn't.

"I am deadly serious. I think you have enormous potential, Sonia, but I understand it would be a big life decision to make."

Her heart was beating very fast as she allowed herself to briefly visualise being at his side in some utopian alternate life.

"Enormous potential? Why thank you, kind sir."

She stood to continue dressing, deliberately facing away in case he saw the excitement in her eyes and then extinguished it by revealing his words to be a cruel joke. Perhaps sensing this, he also stood and by placing his hands on her shoulders he spun her around to face him.

"I'm being serious, but you might not be so keen if you really knew me," he said and she felt his piercing stare that seemed to penetrate her soul. At that moment she felt unable to continue her pretence any longer.

"I know exactly who you are, I've known from the start. Your mother may not watch the television but I do," she confessed. Her heartbeat was now raised more in fear than excitement as she awaited his response.

Avery pulled her close in a firm embrace, using the advantage of his height to look over her shoulder, scanning the room for a potential improvised murder weapon.

"And what exactly do you know and who have you shared that with?" he asked calmly.

"That you're that policeman, Paul Avery, and with everything that happened last year," she said and he felt her trembling body accompany the revelation. "And I haven't told a soul," she quickly added.

Avery felt confident she was telling the truth and postponed any homicidal intent on his part. Instead he felt a strange mixture of pleasure and curiosity, realising he had underestimated the enigma that was Sonia. They both sat down together and Sonia, relieved of the burden of her secret, explained that she had initially agonised as to what to do but as time progressed had been increasingly drawn to Avery.

"I think you're a very intelligent man and must have had reasons for doing what you did. I know the television and newspapers twist things so I wanted to make my own mind up. I believe that fate brings you together with the person you are meant to be with," she explained as he listened silently, occasionally nodding for her to continue.

When the explanation was finished it was met with a smile from Avery and relief flooded through her.

"I think the most important thing going forward is trust, Sonia. Do you trust me?"

"Totally," she said without hesitation.

"Okay, this is moving faster than I had anticipated," said Avery, vocalising his thoughts. "Because of my situation and to ensure we can both move onto a new life together, I would need unquestioning loyalty and support. Can you give me those things, Sonia?"

She felt exhilarated at the prospect of serving him and gave an unequivocal affirmation.

"And what if the things I asked you to do were outside the law or dangerous?" he asked, simultaneously taking hold of both her hands.

"I trust you completely," she replied.

"And if I asked you to hurt someone for me?" he probed.

"I would assume they deserved it," she replied earnestly.

"And if I asked you to kill someone? Could you actually take another person's life for me?"

"Yes, I would do that without hesitation," she replied.

Then much to his delighted surprise she unexpectedly added a comment to corroborate her assertion.

"I have already killed someone."

CHAPTER 9

His trips to Scotland had continued to remain a secret from everyone except Mary and Cameron McKenzie. This was his fourth visit and once again he used a combination of public transport and hire vehicles to reach his destination in the quiet countryside south of Dumfries. His surveillance-conscious method of transport and route were primarily designed to frustrate colleagues as to his whereabouts. It also provided him some reassurance that were Avery still alive he would not be jeopardising the existence of his son Cameron.

For her part Mary McKenzie had reluctantly allowed the visits to take place, but only if Bare adhered to her strict conditions. Those centred on Cameron not being told of his biological connection to the visiting police officer and the nature of the visits not being disclosed to her extended family. Bare was happier with the second condition more than the first as the wider McKenzie family were still an active Organised Crime Group. Mary herself had retired to concentrate on the welfare of her grandson, Cameron.

The previous visits had been of a day's duration but this would be an overnight stay at a local hotel due to the practicalities of travel and to allow a few extra paternal visitation hours. Cameron unquestioningly accepted the visits were part of a police officer's job due to the traumatic experience the pair had shared the previous year. Whilst the house was very comfortable having been funded by Mary's OCG retirement plan, it was somewhat remote, so Cameron viewed Bare as a welcome visitor to play football with in the oversized garden.

Bare in turn hoped that frequent visits would gradually build the trust between him and Mary until perhaps she accepted that Cameron would benefit from the truth about his conception. He knew that this was a very long-term strategy and was content with that, not wishing to destabilise what was clearly a loving relationship between grandmother and grandson.

As part of his tradecraft Bare initially drove past the property whilst making a quick check that none of the pre-arranged signs to abort the mission were in place. These amounted to the strategic placement of a garden ornament which signalled whether Mary already had visitors. After turning around two miles down the road the reciprocal route also allowed him to check out the possibility of any vehicles following him on the remote country road. As he pulled into the long driveway of the property he saw that one of the garage doors had been deliberately left open for him and he parked the hire vehicle immediately inside. After closing the garage door he walked around to the front door which opened as he approached.

He was greeted by the onrushing Cameron whilst Mary remained with her arms folded in the doorway. Cameron and Bare exchanged their customary 'high five' greeting but, before words could be exchanged, Bare saw something in his peripheral vision that made him take a step backwards. Running at full speed from the far side of the house came a snarling Doberman dog on a mission to intercept the visitor. As Bare instinctively raised his palms in a protective gesture he heard Cameron shout an authoritative command.

"Tyrus, close."

Much to Bare's relief the dog made a subtle diversion away from him at the last second before sitting obediently at the boy's side. Cameron gently patted the dog's head and praised him for adhering to the command.

"Bare, we've got a dog," said the excited boy as he continued to fuss the dog whose demeanour had changed from fierce protector to cuddly pet.

"So I see," said Bare, slowly regaining his composure before noticing that the expression on Mary's face indicated she had enjoyed witnessing the introduction.

"Cameron is a very good trainer," were her first words as she belatedly greeted Bare herself.

"Yes, I think he just saved my life," replied a half-joking Bare.

He followed her into the house and straight into the large kitchen where a kettle was already boiling, presumably switched on by his host as he had pulled into the driveway. Mary walked across to it and poured the water into two mugs that had also clearly been prepared for his anticipated arrival.

"I suppose I should have got something stronger in to celebrate your promotion," she said whilst pouring some milk into each of the drinks.

Bare was about to challenge her concerning the origin of that information before remembering he himself had divulged it in an earlier telephone conversation. He had mentioned it for no other reason than to suggest he ought to be financially contributing to Cameron's upbringing but Mary had once again dismissed the suggestion. Instead they had compromised with an agreement that Bare would pay into a savings account that would assist a projected university education in the distant years ahead.

"Coffee is fine, I can't drink and drive as I think it's even frowned upon in Scotland these days," said Bare.

"Oh, yes, and your powers don't extend this far so it would be HMP Barlinnie for you. It's no place for a Sassenach polis," she teased.

After noticing that Cameron and Tyrus had already gone off to play Bare enquired as to the boy's welfare and was gratified to hear that he was doing well.

"The dog is a good idea. I had one at his age and they're wonderful companions," Bare commented.

"Aye and he would be a vicious bastard toward anyone having a go at Cameron," she replied, betraying the real reason for the dog's acquisition.

"I wouldn't imagine you have any worries on that score, they would have to get past his grandma first," replied Bare.

"I take it his bones haven't washed up on any beach yet then?" she asked, ignoring Bare's observation.

"No, I don't suppose they ever will," he replied recognising the familiar content of their conversation.

"Part of me really hopes he is still alive, just so I could make him suffer before finishing the job," she said, sipping her coffee.

The return of boy and faithful hound prevented Bare from answering, but he was in no doubt that Mary McKenzie was speaking quite literally.

CHAPTER 10

If she had ever been implicated in the death her defence could have been that it was a mercy killing, but in truth it was not. Whilst her mother had a long-term illness it would not have naturally shortened her expected lifespan to any great degree. The simple fact was that Sonia had grown tired of her mundane existence and had taken it upon herself to change things. Without any great deal of pre-planning or preparation she had smothered her with a pillow and to her enduring surprise had felt no remorse whatsoever. The sleeping old woman barely had time to offer even the slightest resistance to the murderous act and within less than a couple of minutes was dead.

Sonia had then calmly tidied up before walking into the kitchen to make two cups of tea. The first she sipped slowly whilst listening to the local radio. She wondered if she would be sent to prison but thought even that would be a welcome change from the onerous duty of care she had been performing without complaint for the preceding years. After enjoying the calm of her surroundings for as long as she could she took the second cup through to her mother's room and placed it on the bedside cabinet.

She wasn't sure whether the situation justified use of the '999' system so instead rang her local doctor's surgery which was less than a quarter of a mile away. After explaining that she was struggling to rouse her mother she was advised to call an ambulance which she duly did. To her surprise her own GP, alerted by a concerned receptionist who had taken the original call, arrived before the ambulance to offer assistance. After examining her mother he had confirmed that she had indeed 'passed' and consoled Sonia with the fact that it would have been a peaceful process in her sleep. As he had examined the poor woman only the previous week and diagnosed a chest infection he was even happy to certify the death himself. Sonia learned this would obviate the need for a post mortem and the only words directed at her were full of condolence rather than condemnation.

Within a few weeks the funeral had taken place, the ashes had been scattered and no police had ever knocked on her door to lead her away in handcuffs. She should of course have started a new exciting life at that point but she simply didn't know how to. She knew she was in danger of becoming a recluse with no purpose so when it became evident that Mrs Warner needed the assistance of a regular carer she stepped in to fill the void. As the need for care accelerated she accepted that it was just nature's cruel act of revenge and that this was her destiny.

CHAPTER 11

Avery liked the setup at the self-storage facility where Michael Warner had rented a unit for a number of years. Access was unrestricted, it was safe, secure and largely an anonymous experience visiting the unit. Once he had gained entry he quickly inspected the position of each item of surplus furniture he had acquired over the years to justify the rental. The only purpose of the items was to alert him whether anyone had been inside and to camouflage the small box containing some personal possessions. Satisfied that everything was in place he quickly located and opened the wooden box. Amongst the contents was a small collection of police warrant cards 'lost' by former colleagues over the years. He selected two and placed them in his jacket pocket. He also took the handcuffs together with their leather pouch and two of the six 'burner' phones. He momentarily also picked up the tightly rolled collection of banknotes but then replaced them. The money represented the last of his savings and now that he was being supported by two women in his life, could remain as his absolute emergency fund. Whilst moving the money he did, however, notice and subsequently retrieve the very expensive bottle of wine that lay in its own wooden casket on a bed of straw for additional protection. Although the seal around the cork appeared intact Avery had previously used an extremely thin syringe to inject the contents with an additional deadly liquid. He had done so as an experiment but was now visualising a use for the poison. Lastly he retrieved his remaining stock of Rohypnol and hoped that its long-term storage was not detrimental to its effectiveness.

Satisfied that he had everything he needed he walked backward to the door to reinforce his view of how everything was arranged. After a brief check that his exit would not coincide with any neighbour arrivals he left the unit and walked briskly to the car where Sonia was waiting.

This was to be her first very minor test, an accompanied visit into the town to purchase a couple of decent hunting knives. The revelation concerning how she had become a relatively recent orphan had convinced him that she could be trusted to do his bidding. This was new territory for him as he had always lived a solitary existence when planning and executing murders in the past and he was curious to know whether a shared experience would somehow intensify it.

The shopping excursion turned out to be a brief one as the items were obtained relatively easily. The adrenaline rush of walking past a couple of uniformed police officers was an unexpected bonus and reinforced his belief that he had become 'yesterday's news' which suited him fine.

When they arrived home they silently walked upstairs to avoid waking his surrogate mother who was sleeping soundly in her favoured armchair. They took turns to be photographed by each other against the hastily assembled plain curtain backdrop he had made. He quickly viewed the digital images on the camera and seemingly satisfied, he transferred them across to his computer. After some minimal editing they were ready and the small printer sprang into life to produce the passport-size hard copies.

Sonia studied her own image and commented that she looked very stern and Avery made her laugh by mimicking her furrowed brow. She loved these rare moments of shared humour. He then took the retrieved warrant cards from his pocket and painstakingly eased apart the plastic sides with a craft knife in order to remove the original owner's photographs. Nowadays warrant cards had the photographs digitally embedded but these ones in their small holders, replete with metal crests, looked more authentic than their replacements. After inserting the recently printed photographs and resealing the edges Avery ceremoniously handed her new identification to Sonia.

This was the only thing he had ever given her and she loved the shiny badge displays as she theatrically flicked it open with one hand.

"Stop where you are, police," she asserted whilst practising the action.

"Yes, we may need to work on that," laughed Avery.

Sonia then studied the writing that surrounded her photograph and realised not only did she have a new profession but a new name to learn too.

"Hello, I am Detective Sergeant Winters," she announced whilst holding her identification up for Avery to inspect.

"And I am Detective Inspector Smith," he replied and was a little disappointed that he had not acquired the card from someone with a more glamorous name.

Sonia reluctantly returned the warrant card to Avery for safe keeping and then obeyed his instruction to sit beside him as he opened another piece of software on his computer. She saw that he was formatting a CV and was surprised to see her name at the top.

"I need you to take on a small part-time role I've seen advertised," he explained, whilst fabricating a relevant career history.

CHAPTER 12

As father and son kicked the football to each other Bare realised how fond he was becoming of the visits to Scotland. Mary had absented herself to do some gardening in the front, leaving them to practise in the rear garden where Bare had assembled the goal bought for Cameron as a present. Prior to the visit he had found some photographs of himself as ten-year-old boy and didn't need the confirmed DNA results to know the parentage of Cameron. Mary had told him that the death of her own sons made her determined that Cameron would never follow the same path. By the same token Bare had made the rather tongue-in-cheek comment that he would do his best to deter the lad from a career in law enforcement as well.

With the afternoon sun beating down and the boy laughing uncontrollably at his effort to do 'keepy-uppys', Bare felt more relaxed than he had for a very long time. It was at that moment that perhaps some cruel god decided that happiness was a transient state for Detective Inspector Bare as he heard the scream from the front garden.

Tyrus emerged from the back door having also been alerted by the cry and Bare instinctively reverted from doting dad to police officer.

"Cam, wait here with your dog, do not come around the front," he instructed and the boy immediately complied by calling Tyrus to his side.

Bare reached inside his pocket before remembering his habit of switching off his phone en route to Scotland and leaving it in his car for emergency use only. Realising stealth was his only advantage he kept close to the side of the house as me made his way around to the front. When he got to the final corner he paused briefly to take a deep breath, bracing himself for whatever might be waiting for him.

A quick look provided an initial scene assessment. A set of small metal steps were on their side and a rueful looking Mary McKenzie was sitting at the bottom of a partially cut hedge miraculously still holding a set of pruning shears. A scan of the surroundings suggested there had been no third-party involvement and Bare let out an audible sigh before rushing over to offer assistance.

"I've hurt my knee, help me up," she said, dropping the shears and offering an outstretched hand.

Bare helped her to her feet before asking what had happened.

"For a detective you're not very bright. I fell off the bloody steps, that's what happened," she snapped, but her mood instantly changed as she saw Cameron and his dog emerge apprehensively into the garden.

"Are you okay, Grandma?" asked the boy.

Bare was about to reprimand the boy for not obeying his instruction but then saw the look on his face and in an instant was transported back to the perilous cliff ledge they had shared the previous year.

"She's fine, Cam, I told her not to do gymnastics at her age but would she listen?"

With that, Mary gave him a playful punch in the arm and the tension around immediately dissipated as they all laughed.

It was a natural presumption that the laughter triggered the barking of an excited dog whose collar was being firmly held by Cameron. In reality it was because the dog had sensed the presence of a man silently retreating from his covert vantage point on the other side of the garden hedge.

CHAPTER 13

It felt good to be on the verge of a new kill. He didn't mind the solitary wait for her arrival home, the anticipation running through his veins was a welcome but long overdue visitor. He had contemplated involving Sonia but that would have meant adjusting his long-considered plan and selfishly he wasn't prepared to do that. She would have her uses soon enough but for now it was all about experiencing that intoxicating feeling of absolute power.

Avery checked his watch and knew that if she followed the same routine he had been observing, the new BMW car would be arriving home soon. Her bedroom at the front of the house provided the best observation point and would still give him ample time to get downstairs whilst she parked in the garage at the property.

Right on schedule Amelia Hann arrived home. She pulled onto the driveway and left her car running as she alighted in order to open the garage door. The car stereo was at high volume and the sounds of the Electric Light Orchestra punctuated the otherwise silent cul-de-sac where she lived. Having carefully manoeuvred her pride-and-joy vehicle through the narrow unforgiving aperture of the garage, she once again got out and this time locked it.

He waited until she closed the front door before emerging behind her and swiftly placing his leather-gloved hand over her mouth to stifle any scream. The bright gleam of the large hunting knife held in his other hand became the focus of her terrorised expression as she heard a male voice command her to be quiet. Within seconds she was expertly frogmarched into her small study and made to sit on a waiting chair. He stood behind her and the knife was now being held to her throat. The sensation of the cold steel on her skin was making her shake with fear although intuitively she knew this had to be controlled to avoid being cut.

"I'm going to take my hand away from your mouth. If you scream, I will kill you. I hope you understand this because there are no second chances," Avery said in a calm and authoritative voice designed to make her compliant.

The study was a small interior box room in the centre of the ground floor; it had no windows and was furnished normally with just an office desk and chair. The addition of one of her dining room chairs made the room feel crowded and she immediately realised that its placement meant it was always the burglar's intention to bring her in there. He was still standing behind her so she had no view of his face but could tell he was considerably taller and stronger than her given the ease with which he had moved along her hallway.

"The only money I have is in my purse and my husband will be home any moment so you should take it and go quickly," she heard herself say in a calm voice she barely recognised as her own.

"Well unless you've married someone this afternoon, Miss Hann, I very much doubt that's true," said Avery and took a step to one side, allowing her to look up and see his face for the first time. His groomed facial hair and shaven head were an incongruous match to his refined voice so it took her a few seconds before she recognised him.

"I thought you were dead," she finally stammered.

"Well if it could happen to Lazarus why not to 'Britain's most evil cop' as well?" came the rhetorical reply.

"Are you going to kill me?" she said, unable to avert her gaze from the new face of the man she had written about for weeks on end.

"That's not the question I was expecting from an investigative journalist like yourself, Amelia, I thought you would ask me something broader about my intentions," said Avery, enjoying the encounter as much as he had anticipated.

"What do you want? Why are you here?" she managed to ask.

"That's better, Amelia, open questions designed to get a fuller response rather than a simple binary answer. Well as you asked, I am here to set the record straight, to give you some context to your recent publication that I am afraid to say I felt was underwhelming."

"I just reported the story told to me. There was nothing personal." Her response tailed off as she was fearful of saying anything to provoke the serial killer in her presence.

To her surprise Avery sat down opposite her but he continued to hold the knife close to her upper torso. She quickly realised that any struggle would most likely result in her receiving fatal stab wounds so hoped her conversational skills might keep her alive. She also noticed for the first time there were two full wine glasses on her desk. Noticing her look in that direction Avery smiled.

"Yes, that was a bit rude of me to open one of your collection in the kitchen but I hoped you would join me in a drink. It might calm the nerves."

He motioned toward the glass and unwilling to do anything to antagonise him, she took a reluctant sip.

"So did you ever consider how much better your book would have been had you had the opportunity to interview the man central to it?" he asked.

"Of course, but that was never an option considering you were, well, dead," she replied.

"Well, let's make a start on the revised addition. What do you want to know?" said Avery, before taking her silence as an opportunity to sip his own wine.

CHAPTER 14

Having almost fully recovered from her earlier tumble, Mary cooked the evening meal. Noticing her limp across the kitchen, Bare had offered to assist but had been banished from the room having managed to drop some of the food on the floor. The accident had at least endeared him to the grateful Tyrus whose habit was to lurk in that area just in case that might occur.

Mary studiously ignored the wall-mounted photograph of her late husband as she carried the meals slowly into the dining room. She remained embarrassed about the earlier episode in the garden and was determined to ignore the pain emanating from her swollen ankle. The meal was a simple one but gratefully received by father and son who had worked up an appetite during the competitive football match they had managed before bad light stopped play.

After the meal she had acquiesced to Bare's insistence that he and Cameron would jointly tackle the washing up and she smiled at the sound of her grandson's laughter brought on by an impromptu battle involving the proliferation of soap suds. She was genuinely pleased and proud in equal measure about the way he was growing up, with no sign of the adverse character traits she had seen in her own sons.

This was emphasised further as he retired to bed without complaint when she reminded him that tomorrow was a school day and he ought to get his rest. Bare sat alone in the lounge whilst Mary kissed Cameron goodnight upstairs. He surveyed the array of family photographs on display and wondered how many revolutions per second his presence was causing the McKenzie graves to spin.

He heard Mary approach the lounge and prepared to thank her for the meal before his departure to the nearby hotel for the night. However, when she entered the room he saw she was carrying two glasses of the same red wine they had enjoyed with the meal.

"Seemed silly to put the cork back in," she explained, handing him one of the glasses. The angle of his view from the sofa meant he was looking at her ample cleavage as she bent down to pass him the glass. Any chance that she had missed his instinctive stare was quickly removed by her unconcerned commentary.

"You enjoying the view of those Scottish mountains?" she asked, delighting in the uncomfortable blush he was suffering.

He quickly changed the subject back to that of Cameron's wellbeing and enquired whether his school were fully cognisant of everything that had occurred the previous year. Mary stated they were and felt that it was a safe and nurturing environment for him.

"Would you mind if I took him in tomorrow and maybe just double checked their security protocols?" asked Bare as nonchalantly as he could.

"Security protocols? Do you think he is still out there, Sebastian?" she said, seizing on his words with suspicion.

"No, course not, just nice to have that additional reassurance as I'm normally so far away," he said, trying to quell any rising anxiety.

"Aye, well I'm sure that would be fine then," she said and patted his leg in gratitude.

Bare enjoyed her tactile response and immediately felt conflicted whilst trying to interpret whether it was any more than an inconsequential touch. His train of thought was interrupted by Tyrus transitioning from a slumbering dog to a frenzied barking beast. The dog ran to the back door giving a clear indication that it wished to go outside in pursuit of whatever or whoever was there.

"It's probably just a fox," said Mary, rising to her feet and slowly walking toward the door despite her frenetic animal's insistence that she move quicker.

As she opened the door the dog wasted no time in sprinting outside and the could hear him announce his presence with a series of loud barks. Not wishing the noise to disturb her grandson Mary hissed the dog's name in a reproachful tone in a futile effort to get him to quieten down.

"Have you got a torch?" asked Bare, sufficiently concerned to join Mary at the open doorway.

She left him peering into the dark garden as she went to find one. His only point of reference was the noise still being made by the out-of-sight dog. With newly acquired torch in hand he then walked slowly outside after telling Mary to stay inside and guard the wine. Bare located the dog jumping up at part of a large perimeter wall that was too tall for either of them to scale. Anxious to see what might be on the other side Bare walked further around until he came to the rear gate which he noted was bolted at both the top and bottom. He opened the gate and walked along the exterior wall until he came to the point where the dog had been so frantic.

At this point he found what was left of an old tree trunk that had decayed over the years but was still intact enough for him to climb onto and thereby provide a perfect vantage point over the wall and back toward the house. Even without binoculars that would have accompanied him had he been doing surveillance, he could see that the position gave a view of the brightly lit lounge through its picture window. After clambering down he made a search of the immediate area as best he could by torchlight before returning to the house.

Mary was standing at the same window he had observed and he reported that he had been unable to locate the source of the dog's discontent. Tyrus had followed him back into the house and appeared to be in a much calmer state as Mary gently rebuked him for the disturbance. As she did so Bare drew the heavy curtains across the window to limit any future surveillance opportunities. He was about to vocalise a suggestion but Mary beat him to it.

"It seems silly you going to that hotel only to return in the morning, you may as well sleep here."

"Yes, I guess I could if you don't mind, I have had a couple of wines," he replied to justify the suggestion without alerting her.

"I don't mind, but just to be clear, Sebastian, the only male that sleeps in my bedroom is Tyrus," she said with a playful wag of her finger.

Her flirtation was lost on him as he felt unsettled but nevertheless habit made him reply in a similar tone.

"Lucky Tyrus," he replied.

CHAPTER 15

As she listened to his story the journalist became less frightened about her own personal safety. She realised that the book she had been so proud of was indeed a superficial account of Avery's life. In her publication she had asserted that he had been responsible for six murders and three further attempts. Avery, however, was giving her a chronological history of his life and had already surpassed those numbers before his twenty-fifth birthday. He paused to take another sip of wine and she instinctively mirrored his action whilst wondering whether to ask questions or just wait for him to continue. Sensing her uncertainty, Avery paused his history.

"I'm happy to take questions as we go along," he said. This was the first time in his life that he had told his story and the memories that it was evoking caused him more pleasure than the delightful merlot that was lubricating his vocal chords.

"It seems that you were able to justify each murder to yourself before committing it, was that important to you?" asked Amelia.

Avery had been unprepared for the question, expecting one centred around the events rather than the psychology around them. He paused and gave due consideration before answering.

"I suppose that knowing there was a rationale caused a distinction. Otherwise they would be the random acts of a madman."

"But surely you can appreciate that there is no justification in doing what you did?" came the instant supplementary question, and she immediately regretted asking it in case it provoked an angry response.

Instead Avery was calmness personified as he again thought carefully before giving his very measured answer.

"I think there is a commonly held misconception that unless your acts and thoughts conform to the rules of society then you must be wrong. I don't consider anything I have ever done to be wrong. I recognise that I am judged as a psychopath but that is a lazy description applied by unintelligent morons."

Amelia merely nodded to show an understanding of his view. The way he had ended his sentence with the term 'morons' was, she felt, an early indication of a rising temper she was very keen to avoid.

Avery checked his watch and was disappointed to see how quickly time was passing before returning to his life story. He made sure he was studying her facial micro expressions as he recounted each salacious detail. He could tell she was trying to remain impassive like a true journalist would but equally knew that each additional word was causing shockwaves.

He had barely begun talking about the demise of Julia Bare when he saw the heavy eyelids of Amelia began to close. He was annoyed that he had miscalculated the dosage of Rohypnol in her wine but knew it was futile to continue as she would be unconscious in a few seconds.

He waited for the inevitable slump in her chair before lifting Amelia and carrying her through the house and into the garage. He placed her in the boot of her own car before returning to the house to tidy up and replace everything back in its rightful place. He took particular care to wash the wine glasses and replace them in the kitchen cabinet where he had originally found them, whilst waiting for her to arrive.

He then replicated the manner in which she left the house each day by driving her car onto the driveway and closing the garage door behind him. It was now early evening and the darkness was his friend in case anyone happened to be passing, but he saw no one. The drive to the woods where he had already prepared her grave took less than fifteen minutes and he used the time to listen to the local news on her car radio.

Upon arriving at the deposition site he made torchlight inspection of the camouflaged grave and only when satisfied there had been no changes since he left it did he open the boot. She was now in that halfway state between conscious and unconscious; her eyes were open but the power of speech and movement were still lost. He searched for some understanding in her eyes that might have compensated for her missing the final chapters of his story but was only met with a blank stare. Her ornate silver necklace that had a silver 'A' on it was carefully removed by Avery and placed into his pocket.

He dropped her into the grave as if fly-tipping some inconvenient waste and stared down at her prone body before returning to the vehicle to retrieve the item he had brought from her study. It was her own copy of the publication that had ultimately led to her death and he tossed it down to join her. Then he used the earlier concealed shovel to fill in the grave, knowing that the weight and density of the earth would suffocate her within a short period of time. There was a probability the identity of her killer would be easily identified should her body be discovered but that was not important to him. The link between him and her disappearance would not be immediately obvious enough to warrant a full alert and would allow him the breathing space to continue his plans. He smiled at the irony of his own thoughts in the knowledge that breathing space was the one thing Amelia Hann was desperately lacking.

He then drove her car back to her house, stopping only to throw the shovel into some shallow water of a roadside ditch. Apart from some timing issues things had worked out pretty much as he had planned. He felt invigorated and part of him wanted to fast forward to the final act of his plan before he took some deep breaths and reminded himself that this time would be different. This time he would be in complete control.

CHAPTER 16

After dropping Cameron off at the school and using the opportunity to have a constructive meeting with the headteacher, Bare started the long journey home. A daylight inspection of the perimeter wall had reassured him that any suspicions that they had been subject to surveillance the previous night were probably misplaced and more likely to be a result of his paranoia than anything else.

This had been the best visit by far and he felt there was a growing bond between him and Cameron. He also felt there was a growing bond between him and Mary McKenzie but hoped that was more to do with alcohol than any specific intent on her part. The recollection of the brief sexual tension between them the previous evening did make him smile and verbally chastise himself as he drove along the quiet road.

He hoped that the various public transport component parts of his journey would enable him to make it back in time for the promised late shift, although he knew he would be cutting it fine. To be fair this was just going to be a 'moving office' day and greeting his new team, so hopefully nobody would be too critical of his timeliness.

The solitary journey afforded him a lot of thinking time which he didn't always welcome but for the first time in a very long time he was allowing a little positivity to creep into his mindset. He checked his watch and made a mental note to call Robin during her lunch hour. It was still very early days in their relationship and he wondered at what point he would have to tell her about Cameron. Almost shuddering at the prospect, he dismissed the idea by reassuring himself that was still a distant future dilemma.

When he arrived at the police station he was disappointed to find that Brady was out. The box containing his belongings was still stored in the corner of what had been his office until she had assumed occupancy. Now that he knew where his new role was to be based he picked it up and trudged toward the lift. The weight of the box made it an awkward carry but that was still preferable to the red tape involved delegating the task to whatever department now line managed the caretakers. Indeed it was a familiar sight on 'moves and postings' day to see a confusion of middle managers similarly laden as they passed each other in the corridor en route to their new position.

He knew the majority of the staff working in the CIB already although was thankful that the support staff member who first greeted his arrival was diligently wearing his name badge.

"Welcome to the Compliance and Intelligence Bureau, sir," said the data analyst, rising from his chair and offering an outstretched hand.

"Thanks Andy," replied Bare, still feeling slightly embarrassed at his transition from 'sarge' to 'sir'.

It was apparent that that the majority of CIB dayshift workers had already concluded their work and disappeared for the day so mercifully there were only a few more introductory handshakes before he located his new office. His predecessor had already retired from the Constabulary before Bare's appointment so there was no formal handover of work. Instead a brief note had been left for him containing a few hastily scribbled words from his new Sergeant who had been covering the position in an 'Acting' capacity. The note finished with an apology that the Sergeant was now on annual leave so wouldn't actually meet his new boss for a couple of weeks.

Bare leant back in his office chair and took stock of his new surroundings. The role was 99% office based so he guessed he would have to get used to the twelve square feet he had been allocated. Already feeling quite claustrophobic he decided to explore the department or, to be accurate, locate the communal kitchen area in search of caffeine. Upon entering the tiny area he realised that each staff member had their own labelled 'stash' of tea and coffee. Years of experience had taught him that to appropriate anyone else's ingredients without permission was tantamount to a hanging offence. He concluded that he would have to undertake a journey to the main canteen; so much for 'rank has its privileges'.

As he was about to leave the annoyingly cheerful Andy appeared at the doorway alongside a female whose 'uniform' suggested she was a cleaner.

"Oh, sir, can I introduce you to someone else who is starting here today?" said Andy, gesturing unnecessarily in the direction of the new staff member.

"Hi, DI Sebastian Bare," he said, introducing himself.

"Pleased to meet you, I'm Sonia," came the nervous reply.

CHAPTER 17

The third floor of the police station was eerily quiet apart from the sound of her other colleague's vacuum cleaner. It was 6.30am and she remembered he had told her that staff working on that floor rarely arrived before 8 o'clock. Nevertheless, she walked past the office several times before tentatively opening the door. His description of the room was incredibly accurate and she had no difficulty in locating the box file he had told her to find. She double checked the label on the front which read 'Low risk RSO visits' before removing the contents and spreading the papers on the floor. This enabled her to quickly photograph the papers with her phone before meticulously returning them to the file in the same order that she had removed them.

Her heart was beating fast as she was not used to committing acts of espionage and she slowly emerged from the office. Such was her focus on the assigned task she had failed to notice that the noise of her colleague's cleaning had ceased.

"We don't have to clean in there," said Cheryl, pointing to the room from where Sonia had just emerged.

Such was the shock of the intervention Sonia almost dropped her phone in fright before she managed to mumble some form of incoherent apology. Much to her relief Cheryl did not appear at all suspicious about her actions but instead took the opportunity to educate her new colleague about the geography of the station.

"That's the Public Protection Officer's room," she said.

"Oh, right. What do they do?" asked Sonia, sensing Cheryl was keen to impart her considerable knowledge built up over years of working for the Constabulary.

"They have to keep tabs on all those horrible sex offenders. Do you know how many of them live in the town? Have a guess!"

"I don't know, is it a lot?" Sonia replied.

Despite the absence of anyone else on the entire floor Cheryl leaned forward to whisper the answer she had been reliably informed was correct by one of the admin staff some weeks earlier.

"Nearly two hundred of the buggers," was her outraged insight. "I am telling you, if the public only knew there would be questions asked."

"That's shocking," said Sonia and then as an afterthought, "I guess it just proves you don't know who is out there."

CHAPTER 18

Sharon Brady read the commentary on the report for the third time and felt a growing sense of unease. By coincidence just as she finished, its author walked past her office.

"Jasmin, have you got a second?" she called out, hoping that PC Khan was still in audible range.

"Of course, Sarge, how can I help?" said the junior officer, reappearing in the doorway.

"I'm just reviewing your Mispers report from last week, Amelia Hann. It seems very unusual."

"Yes, it's weird, Sarge. She didn't turn up for work on Monday morning and her boss couldn't get hold of her, her phone goes straight to voicemail. When she didn't turn up the next day either he reported it," said the young officer, excited by the interest in one of her cases.

"And what enquiries have been done so far?" asked Brady, recognising the inexperience that was very evident in PC Khan's demeanour.

"Well I went to her address and there was no reply so I did a bit of house-to-house but there was nothing useful. So I went back to her boss and got Amelia's next of kin details and from that I went to see her mum. She didn't know anything either but I got the impression they are not particularly close. Anyway she wasn't particularly worried and said Amelia was probably away researching a story."

Brady's unease grew further as the officer related a few more superficial enquiries that had been conducted. It was a sad fact that reduced staffing levels combined with an ever increasing workload meant that a number of cases failed to get the attention they deserved and she was fearful that there had been some glaring omissions in this instance.

Belatedly sensing some constructive criticism was coming her way, PC Khan explained that this was her first solo missing person enquiry and she had sought advice from her Acting Sergeant who had offered little by way of guidance.

Upon hearing the identity of the officer covering the leave period of PC Khan's substantive supervisor, Brady felt a wave of empathy for the young officer. Nevertheless, the words of her own initial Sergeant and long-time role model came crashing to the forefront of her mind and she couldn't help but vocalise them.

"Okay, Jasmin, we need to get a grip of this as it's got the potential to bite us on the arse. You'd better drive me to Hann's house so we can make a proper scene assessment."

"No problem, Sarge. I did wonder if CID would get interested given the book Amelia Hann wrote."

It was only at that point that the vague familiarity of the missing person's name fully resonated with Brady.

"Oh shit, she's that journalist that wrote about Paul Avery," Brady said, full of self-recrimination for not making the connection earlier.

"Yes. Should I have put that in the report, Sarge? It's just my supervisor said only to include facts relevant to her disappearance."

"We can have a talk en route, Jasmin," said Brady in the fervent hope that it was indeed an irrelevant detail.

CHAPTER 19

Sonia wasted no time in delivering the proceeds of her crime to Avery once her shift had finished. She told him exactly how she had captured the images despite nearly being caught by her co-worker but he appeared disinterested and concentrated on downloading the images to his computer in order to get a better look at them. He quickly scrolled through the records, dismissing each in turn as being unsuitable before he stopped at the penultimate one. After double checking the detail he leaned back in his chair and smiled broadly.

"Oh, you clever girl. This one is perfect," he said, causing her heart to swell with pride even though she didn't really understand what she had done.

"Raymond Archibald Wilson, thirty-five years old, a series of indecent exposures and an all-round horrible little weasel," announced Avery, returning his focus to the screen. "His profile is absolutely perfect and the fact that his name is Raymond is a complete bonus."

"Oh, good," said Sonia, peering at the screen herself. "Is this someone you want to kill?"

Avery laughed at the directness of her question.

"All in good time, Sonia, but for now I want you to give Raymond the best night of his sad little life."

For the rest of the day he helped Sonia rehearse her role, patiently answering every hypothetical question she posed and reminding her he would only be a few seconds away should she need him. Although she had some reservations he convinced her that her actions would be absolutely pivotal to his plan and as they left the house her only concern was that she might let him down.

By the time she knocked on Wilson's door it was early evening. Initially there was no response and she felt a strange combination of relief and disappointment. But then the door was reluctantly opened and she met Raymond Wilson.

"Detective Sergeant Winters from the Public Protection Department," announced Sonia, holding up the warrant card for inspection.

"I had my six-monthly visit last month," complained Wilson.

"And you know we sometimes do random follow-ups," she replied with the authority her position required.

Wilson opened the door fully and stood to one side with the weary resignation of a man used to such police scrutiny. He was surprised that the Sergeant appeared to be by herself as such visits were normally undertaken by a pair of officers, but obediently followed her into his flat. She looked around with some disdain at the hovel Wilson called home and wondered what was on the now closed laptop on the coffee table. Wilson followed her gaze and groaned when he realised he had failed to secrete the device prior to opening the door.

"It's not mine, it belongs to a friend," he said apologetically in the full realisation that possession of the laptop was prohibited under the terms of his sex offender registration.

The admission gave Sonia a surge of confidence as she remembered the subservient stance Avery had predicted Wilson would adopt.

"Sit down, Raymond," she commanded and he instantly complied.

She sat next to him on the grubby two-seater sofa which made him instinctively edge as far away as the furniture allowed. He was not used to being alone with a woman and particularly with one who required him to be on his absolute best behaviour. Consequently he desperately tried to avert his eyes as she crossed her legs, allowing him a quite deliberate view of a stocking top as her skirt rode up a few inches.

"I am fairly new in post and have some unconventional methods of keeping offenders on the straight and narrow," she explained.

He didn't really hear her words, however, as his entire focus was on her hand that was now on his tracksuit-covered thigh.

"I believe that if your desires are met in a controlled environment then they won't pop up at unwanted times. Do you agree, Raymond?" she asked as her hand slowly but steadily moved north.

In truth Raymond was already beyond rational thought and could only assume he was either dreaming or about to be the subject of an elaborate police sting operation designed to get him a lengthy custodial sentence. In the fervent hope it was the former rather than the latter, he remained silent.

Fifteen minutes later she emerged from the flat leaving an exhausted and bewildered sex offender on his sofa with his tracksuit bottoms still around his ankles. She tied a knot in the full condom before placing it carefully in the plastic bag Avery was holding open for her.

CHAPTER 20

Despite not being on the best of terms with her daughter it transpired that Amelia Hann's mother still had a spare key for her daughter's house, which the officers had picked up en route. After getting no reply to a prolonged door knock Brady put on some disposable gloves and motioned Jasmin Khan to do the same. She then entered the house and called out Amelia's name in case the house owner was in residence after all. Upon receiving no reply the officers commenced a slow and systematic search of each room in the house. As they did so Brady provided a commentary partly through habit but mostly by way of vocational training for PC Khan.

"Fridge well stocked, unlikely she has left on a planned trip," said Brady, moving slowly around the kitchen whilst trying to obtain a 'sense' of Amelia Hann.

Each room visited told her the same thing. This was the home of a young professional woman, neat and methodical with little evidence of family and associated sentimentality. The displayed artwork was not to Brady's taste; each wall-mounted print appeared to have been picked to blend in rather than make an individual statement.

Brady's growing conclusion was that this was not the home of a person with a disposition for spontaneity, making her apparent sudden disappearance even more concerning. The final interior door led the officers into the integral garage where they found Amelia's car neatly parked, leaving no room for the normal bric-a-brac most people safeguard in that area. Brady recollected seeing some keys hanging in the kitchen and requested the junior office retrieve them whilst she checked the exterior of the vehicle. The car appeared undamaged, albeit slightly dirtier than she would have expected given the almost obsessive cleanliness of the house interior.

Brady used the key fob to unlock the vehicle and it obediently flashed its indicators to signal that she could look inside. She opened the driver's door and crouched down beside the car before reaching in to activate the boot release mechanism. She then walked to the rear of the vehicle and opened the boot of the BMW. PC Khan joined her at the rear of the vehicle and emitted an audible sigh of relief upon seeing there was nothing inside.

"For a minute I thought we were going to find a body in there, Sarge," she said.

Brady ignored the comment and was clearly locked into her own thoughts, so Khan made no further attempts to initiate a conversation. Instead she began to open the passenger door of the vehicle to conduct her own inspection. The action caused a quick rebuke from Brady who instructed she close the door and make a call to the on-call Senior Crime Scene Investigator instead.

"Tell him I want a forensic team down here as soon as possible, potential serious crime scene," Brady instructed.

"But why, Sarge, there's no trace of our mispers here?"

"Because something's not right. How tall is Amelia?"

"Err, I can't remember, Sarge. Why?"

"According to the report you completed she's tiny, just over 5 foot tall, and she lives alone."

"Yes, but I don't understand the relevance," replied the confused officer.

"Look at the position of the driver's seat and rear-view mirror, Jasmin. Whoever parked this vehicle is considerably taller. And look in the centre console."

PC Khan peered again into the vehicle and saw the pink mobile phone case with its monogrammed letter 'A'. The design of the case meant it was possible to see the case contained a new-looking mobile phone.

"Tell me what self-respecting journalist would go anywhere without her mobile phone. Get the CSI down here before we lose any more time."

PC Khan immediately complied as Brady left the garage in order to make a private phone call of her own. The number she called was on speed dial meaning she only had to depress a couple of buttons before she heard the ring tone. When he answered she wasted no time with any unnecessary greetings.

"Seb, you will want to know about this," she said and Bare immediately recognised the gravity of her tone.

CHAPTER 21

Eve Kent closed the front door behind her and as part of her daily ritual playfully stuck her tongue out at the CCTV camera gazing protectively over the front aspect of the large detached house. She knew her father was unable to resist monitoring the daily footage of family members' arrivals and departures, interspersed with the odd delivery driver. Like a lot of other teenagers she felt somewhat conflicted about the invasion of her privacy balanced against the need for security, but had grown used to it over the years.

The gravelled driveway was now devoid of vehicles with all the other family members being at work, but last night it had been full, meaning she had to find some on-street parking nearby for her Ford Fiesta car. Although not brand new she had been ecstatic to receive it as an eighteenth birthday present a few months earlier and was now the envy of her college friends. However, finding an available parking space was always a challenge in the heavily populated and affluent residential area where she had lived the majority of her life.

As she arrived at her car she was immediately approached by a smartly dressed couple clearly intent on speaking to her. She removed her ear buds that had been playing at full volume in time to hear their initial question.

"Miss Eve Kent?" enquired the male.

"Who wants to know?" she replied, her refined accent masking the confrontational challenge of her response.

"Detective Inspector Smith and DS Winters," came the instant reply with a simultaneous display of warrant cards.

"Oh, is everything alright?" asked the nervous teenager.

"We're investigating a serious allegation that has been made against you, Miss Kent, and need you to come with us and formally answer some questions."

"What allegation? That's ridiculous. Don't you know who my dad is?" she said with rising indignation.

"Yes of course we do, Miss Kent, that's why we want to do this discreetly with the minimum of fuss. As a concession to you, we can take your vehicle so you leave as soon as we have asked our questions. Your father has been fully briefed, now please give your keys to DS Winters."

The calm, authoritative tone used by Avery ensured immediate compliance and she was ushered into the rear of her own vehicle whilst still trying to formulate a verbal response. She was quickly joined by Avery who sat alongside her and Sonia got into the driver's seat.

With only a small amount of composure regained, Eve took out her mobile phone.

"I need to ring my dad," she announced.

Her attempt to make the call was swiftly interrupted by Avery who took the phone from her hand and turned off the device despite her protestations.

"I'm sorry, miss, but you only be allowed to make a call once you have been documented at the police station. We're not allowed to bend the rules just because of who your dad is."

"I can't believe this is happening. There's going to be hell to pay for this," said Eve, and she grimaced as Sonia made a less than smooth gear change. "God, I thought police officers were taught to be advanced drivers," she complained before looking sullenly out of the window.

The rest of the journey was completed in silence after the officers made it clear they could offer no additional information as to the reasons for her detention until they reached the police station. After a twenty-minute drive the car turned onto a small private road unfamiliar to Eve. It eventually stopped alongside what appeared to be a small anonymous single storey building.

"Where are we?" asked Eve.

"It's one of our covert sites. Your dad didn't want the embarrassment of you being booked in at the main police station. I guess being the daughter of the Assistant Chief Constable has some advantages," explained Avery as he led Eve toward a discreet side door.

CHAPTER 22

Victor Kent had just arrived home when he heard the tone on his phone alerting him that a text message was waiting to be read. He hoped it wasn't a work-related missive as he was looking forward to a relaxing evening watching football on the television accompanied by a large glass of wine. Although he didn't want to wish his time away his impending retirement couldn't come soon enough. He was therefore pleasantly surprised to see the text was from his daughter, but the feeling quickly turned into one of concern as he read the message content.

Help Dad! Got a puncture and don't know how to fix it. Am in big lay-by, A63 just before motorway and phone about to die, text me back if you can rescue me. Hugz E xxx

Kent contemplated ringing her but then realised a call could drain her phone battery even more, so he simply texted back that he would be with her in fifteen minutes. Whilst it was not the most exciting of tasks, Kent relished the diminishing opportunities to be his daughter's hero. She was growing up fast and would undoubtedly soon move on and fall in love with someone he would consider inadequate, so he quickly returned to his car. He knew the location she was referring to but was puzzled as to why she was there. He hoped that she was adhering to all the safety advice he had imparted over the years but consoled himself in the knowledge that he would soon arrive to rescue her.

Avery read the response and was pleased he wouldn't have to wait too long. The location had been selected with care as it afforded him the perfect opportunity to reacquaint himself with ACC Kent. He had witnessed his former boss assume the role of the Constabulary's 'talking head' following last year's events and was keen to deliver some constructive criticism. Kent had adopted the strategy of describing Avery as an inadequate and weak-minded individual who had buckled under the strain of police work. This had, in Kent's esteemed opinion, led to a totally unforeseen mental breakdown by Avery necessitating a swift and decisive response. Of course the leadership of the dynamic ACC had been pivotal to the 'success' of the operation.

The message history between father and daughter had been invaluable in composing the plea for help especially as the increasingly precocious Eve had withdrawn all cooperation upon being handcuffed to a radiator. Avery wondered whether Sonia was enjoying her allocated responsibility as a prison guard. Judging from the glint in her eyes when he left he suspected she was. He wondered how she would interpret his parting message to 'have fun' but resisted the temptation to call her upon realising Kent's arrival could be imminent and it was vital that his timing was perfect.

As Kent pulled into the lay-by he remembered how isolated from the nearby motorway it was. Whilst the entrance and exit were visible from the road the entire 200m length was camouflaged by an island of trees. There had once been a static burger van situated at one end but this had long since departed and the pull-in was now rarely used due to the proximity of gleaming new motorway services less than a mile away.

The eerie near-dusk light made it difficult for him to see definitively whether his daughter's car was occupied as he parked his vehicle behind it. Upon alighting from his own vehicle he was puzzled that this had not prompted the appearance of Eve. More confusing was that there were no obvious sign of any of her tyres being punctured and he wondered if another Samaritan had preceded his arrival. He was about to use his phone to ring her when he saw a lone figure standing in the treeline close to her vehicle. The figure looked taller than his daughter but nevertheless he ventured a hesitant greeting.

"Eve, is that you?"

The figure stepped forward and Kent squinted in order to achieve some better focus in the fading light. It wasn't until the man spoke, however, that Kent fully recognised the man standing in front of him.

"Hello Victor, it's been a long time," greeted Avery.

Kent was unable to formulate a response as the physical shock of the encounter left him with an open-mouthed paralysis. Only the sudden realisation that his daughter's absence was now a thousand times more concerning made him stutter some words.

"Where is my daughter? What have you done, you bastard?"

Instinctively Kent started to make an emergency call but before he had even depressed the first number '9' Avery commanded him to stop.

"If you want to see Eve unharmed I wouldn't do that," he said, pointing to Kent's illuminated phone.

Kent immediately stopped and held up his phone as if to demonstrate his compliance. His mind was a cacophony of confusion as he stared at the man he believed to be dead and wondered what nightmare was about to unfold.

CHAPTER 23

Bare had wasted no time making strides toward Woodham's office and was relieved to see she was there as he walked into the room without even a cursory knock. His dramatic entrance caused her to look up from a report she had been studying and she awaited the imminent explanation that was about to follow.

"Avery is not dead," he announced.

She calmly directed him to sit down before walking across to close the door Bare had left open. She was unsure what was to follow but sensed confidentiality was required. Bare used the few seconds' time granted to take a couple of deep breaths as he felt his elevated heart rate might hamper his ability to speak further.

"Okay, tell me everything," she said, reaching for her A4 'daybook' used to record all things of consequence.

The action made Bare take another deep breath as he recognised the need to be factual given her obvious intention to record his account contemporaneously.

"Sharon Brady has just called in a job. A journalist called Amelia Hann has gone missing in suspicious circumstances. She was the one who serialised what happened last year and authored the book about Avery," he said and realised immediately he had no factual link to his opening remark.

Woodham diligently recorded the information in her book and then raised both eyebrows to indicate Bare should continue.

"It's too much of a coincidence, ma'am," was his inadequate

follow-up.

"I see," said Woodham, slowly closing her book. "No doubt DS Brady is doing all the necessary enquiries regarding Ms Hann?"

"Yes, I think uniform were a little slow out of the blocks but Sharon is there now sorting it, but it's him, ma'am," said Bare.

"Well unless you're going to tell me something else I think it's a bit early to leap to any unlikely conclusion like that, Sebastian," she replied.

The expression on his face betrayed the fact he had no more factual information to provide and he waited for the inevitable instruction that was coming his way.

"Look, Seb, I know after everything that happened last year it's going to be difficult for you and of course it's right to highlight the connection between this missing person and Avery. But I think you will agree that upon reflection it's a tenuous one at best. Besides, your role in CIB means you have no operational involvement in matters like this so take a deep breath and let DS Brady do her job. Hope we understand each other?"

Bare was more annoyed with himself than the response of Woodham, despite the barely concealed patronising tones she employed.

"Of course, ma'am. Sorry to have bothered you," he said.

"No problem at all, completely understandable in your situation," she replied with the sweetest of smiles that did nothing to make him feel better.

He returned to his office at a slower pace and reflected on the information Brady had conveyed. Upon reaching the sanctuary of the CIB he made two calls in quick succession: the first was to Mary McKenzie and the second one was to Robin but the message was essentially the same… 'be very careful'.

Then, unable to concentrate on any of the papers on his desk that were demanding attention, he walked to the window. A large plane passed overhead and it was apparent life was continuing as normal outside. He began to wonder whether the memories that were still so vivid were merely fuelling irrational paranoia. As much as that indicated he had a developing mental health problem, it was still a more reassuring thought than the alternative.

CHAPTER 24

Kent's extreme concern for the welfare of his daughter made him totally compliant when Avery told him to follow him a few yards into the dark wooded area adjacent to the lay-by. Avery was clearly keen that their meeting would not be witnessed by anyone else in the locality, however unlikely that a third car might pull into the quiet unlit area. When Avery stooped to retrieve an item from an earlier concealed bag Kent fully expected to see him brandish a weapon of some description. Instead he was surprised to see Avery was now unscrewing the top of a bottle of scotch.

"If my memory is correct this is your favourite, the one that you keep in your desk drawer," said Avery, offering the open bottle to his former boss.

"Where is Eve?" responded Kent, making no move to accept the drink.

"Eve is alive and well. She is currently with a friend of mine. Now have a drink, Victor, as her continued good health depends on it."

Kent reluctantly took the bottle and for a nanosecond considered using it to strike Avery across the head but instead just stared at the man, searching for some understanding of what was going on. It quickly became apparent that Avery was waiting for him to drink from the bottle before communicating any further so he slowly put it to his lips.

"Don't worry, it hasn't been poisoned. Take a good gulp, Victor, it will calm your nerves," encouraged Avery.

Kent realised that he had little choice so closed his eyes and took a large measure of the alcohol, immediately recognising the familiar warm sensation in his throat.

"That's better. I remember when we first shared a drink in your office, seems like a lifetime ago," reminisced Avery, whilst depressing a button on a mobile phone he had retrieved from his jacket pocket.

Kent heard a brief ringtone and saw that a video connection was being established. Avery held the phone up in such a way that the display screen faced Kent who immediately recognised his daughter on the device.

"Eve, are you okay?" cried Kent.

He saw his daughter squint at the phone that was clearly being held by an unseen third party in front of her. She recognised the voice but was struggling to see any image given the gloom of Kent's surroundings.

"Dad, is that you? What's happening?" came the anguished response.

Kent was unable to offer any insight to his daughter as Avery immediately terminated the call and replaced the handset in his pocket.

"Now I am sure you understand the 'proof of life' concept in kidnappings, Victor, and you are reassured that Eve is unharmed and in my care," said Avery with the calm authority of a man in total control.

"What do you want? Please don't hurt her, she has done nothing wrong," implored Kent.

"I want you to keep drinking, Victor," said Avery, motioning toward the bottle that Kent was now clutching tightly as though it was some sort of improvised comfort blanket.

"I have money, just please don't hurt her," said Kent before taking another large swig of the drink.

"I don't want your money, Victor, just follow me and I will show you exactly how you can keep your daughter safe. And keep drinking!" commanded Avery.

With that, he ushered Kent through some more trees until they emerged at the top of a steep embankment. From their position they had a clear view of the busy motorway below with its almost unbroken stream of fast travelling white lights coming from their right.

"It's a busy road," remarked Avery factually but at the same time offering no explanation as to why he had made Kent follow him to the vantage point.

Kent was confused but recognised the nonverbal cue from Avery to take another drink. This time he spluttered as Avery gently tilted the bottle at its base with his finger.

"What would you do to save your daughter, Victor?" he asked.

"Anything, anything, just tell me what you want," replied an increasingly frantic Kent.

"Listen carefully then. I was very disappointed that in the wake of my departure that you metaphorically – now what's the expression? – threw me under the bus. And all to further your own pathetic career."

"I'm sorry, I'm sorry," mumbled Kent who was by now drinking the whisky freely in an effort to gain favour with the madman who was responsible for his daughter's life.

"Well if that's a true apology I want actions rather than words," said Avery obliquely.

"Just tell me what I can do. It doesn't matter about me, my time is up anyway if I'm honest," pleaded Kent.

Avery looked at his watch and waited a few seconds before making his demand.

"Unless you do exactly what I say, in exactly three minutes Eve's pretty neck will be cut and that gorgeous girl will gurgle her least breath. All you have to do to save her is cross that road with your eyes shut," said Avery, motioning toward the motorway below them.

For a moment Kent stared at the three speeding lanes of traffic uncomprehending before turning back to face his tormenter who was theatrically looking at his watch.

"But why?" was all Kent could manage to ask.

"Two minutes thirty-three seconds," Avery answered.

"It's impossible, I'll be killed," responded Kent.

"If you don't try Eve will die in two minutes eighteen seconds," said Avery.

"How do I know you won't kill her anyway?" cried Kent.

"You have my word, Victor, it's you I want to hurt, not her. Your choice, you or Eve."

In that instant Kent understood what was being demanded. Despite the alcohol starting to have an affect his thought process was crystal clear. If he refused his daughter would die; if he complied she might die anyway but there was a chance Avery would be true to his word. Without another word he took another gulp of the anaesthetising liquor and clambered down the bank to the edge of the road. He looked back up to where he thought Avery was standing but couldn't see him in the dark. He had no doubt, however, that the man was there, watching his every movement.

The tears welled in his eyes as he realised there would be no opportunity to say his planned goodbye to loved ones after all. Without looking he started to walk across the first lane of the motorway and barely made it three yards before the speeding lorry struck him and catapulted his already lifeless body into the air like a grotesque rag doll.

CHAPTER 25

Bare made his way to the police canteen in the hope that Brady would call in there en route back to her office. Woodham had made it abundantly clear that he was not to be involved in the investigation into Hann's disappearance but she had not gone so far as to forbid any contact with the investigating officer so he hoped for an informal debrief over a coffee.

There was a predictably long queue for the selection of hot evening meals on offer but a sudden exodus of yellow fluorescent jacket wearing staff meant he did not have to wait long for his turn to be served. The ever informative cook informed him there had been a major RTC (Road Traffic Collision) on the M12 so consequently there was now an abundance of her delicious lasagne, pre-ordered by traffic officers, on offer.

"So tempting, Doris, but I have turned vegetarian," said Bare with an apologetic shrug of his shoulders.

"Since when?" she said in genuine disbelief. She had an almost encyclopaedic knowledge of her customers' dietary requirements and was appalled she had not been made aware of this development.

"About thirty seconds ago when I saw the state of it," he replied.

She retorted by flicking a garden pea at him which he instinctively caught before throwing it in the air and catching it with his mouth.

"Thought you would have to behave properly now they promoted you," she laughed.

"I know. What on earth were they thinking?" he whispered in a conspiratorial tone.

"Fuck knows!" she replied flatly, trying to disguise her pleasure that one of her favoured officers appeared to be getting back on track.

"I can see that my update has shaken you to the core," he heard Brady say and for the first time realised she had followed him into the canteen.

"Just the person I was hoping to see," said Bare truthfully. "You want a coffee?"

"Yes but as a take-away, I have to go and update Ma'am," she replied.

"And do I get an update too?" he asked.

"Yes but not here, Seb, I have a really bad feeling about this," she replied and her sombre tone immediately resonated with Bare.

"Okay. Text me when you are free and we can meet at the Swan," he said, referring to a local pub they both knew well.

"Okay," she replied and as an afterthought thanked him for the coffee as she hurried out of the canteen.

Bare turned back to pay and was handed a plate of lasagne by Doris.

"You need to keep your strength up, dear," she said with a salacious wink.

"Well it will be like a workout carrying that to the table. I hope you at least use organic cement," replied Bare, pretending to use all his strength to carry the plate away.

CHAPTER 26

It took Avery nearly an hour to return, having disposed of Eve's vehicle on the way. He was curious as to how Sonia had coped in his absence but she looked calm as he entered the room. He saw that Eve had been further restrained with an additional set of handcuffs and she was now gagged. He assumed correctly that Sonia had grown tired of her verbal protestations following the short video call with her father and had applied the scarf to silence Eve's tirade.

"Everything okay?" she enquired.

"Yes, absolutely fine, though the traffic was murder," he replied.

Sonia felt her heartbeat steadily rise as Avery took off his jacket and crouched in front of the prisoner. Eve Kent had moved from a state of fear to wild indignation in his absence fuelled by the realisation that her 'arrest' had been part of a clever plan to extort money from her father. Her only concern was that her tormenters had worn facemasks at the time of her capture but now didn't appear at all concerned about concealing their identity.

Avery stared at her and marvelled at the unconditional love that must have existed to make Kent lay down his own life so obediently earlier. He felt a wave of superiority in the knowledge that he could never be as weak or manipulated as the senior police officer had been.

The continued gaze of Avery unnerved Eve and the confidence she had drawn from her earlier 'understanding' of the situation began to evaporate. Despite her best efforts a solitary tear emerged and began to roll slowly down her face. Avery watched it before gently brushing it away with his gloved hand. He then removed a gold ring from her hand and after briefly inspecting it he slipped into his pocket. Once again her eyes flashed with outrage at the loss of her jewellery that had huge sentimental value.

"I expect you must be wondering what on earth is happening," he said softly.

She tried to respond verbally but the gag prevented any intelligible words coming from her mouth. Avery put his index finger to his own lips to indicate she should remain quiet before turning to Sonia.

"I think Eve would be more comfortable if the gag was removed. Would you cut it off please, Sonia?"

Sonia walked over to her bag to retrieve the knife as Avery stood up.

"It's only fair to tell you what is going on, Eve. You know I have just met your dad and I am afraid that following our meeting he was involved in an awful accident with an articulated lorry."

Her eyes looked up at him imploringly which he took as a request for more detail so he continued.

"If I am honest I think drink was involved, which is reprehensible for a senior police officer but before we parted I did make him a promise."

Eve blinked furiously in an attempt to clear the tears from her eyes as she tried to decipher the cryptic message being delivered.

"I promised your dear father that if he did what I asked of him I wouldn't harm you and I am a man of my word," said Avery.

With that he stepped back and gave the briefest of nods to Sonia. She in turn stepped forward and without hesitation used one hand to grab Eve's hair and violently jerk her head back, thereby extending the girl's neck upwards and toward her. Then just as he had made her practise a hundred times before, she used the knife in her other hand to swiftly cut the carotid artery with a sideways motion.

"Sadly for you, Sonia made no such undertaking," said Avery to Eve's lifeless body.

CHAPTER 27

Bare was the first to arrive at the Swan Public House. Back in the day the weekday evening slot would have seen it wall to wall with off-duty cops unable to navigate past it on their way home from work. Bare wondered how many incidents of post-traumatic stress disorder had been averted by the informal debriefings that were then so commonly part of the police family culture. He had witnessed many a shell-shocked colleague walk in following attendance at a horrific crime scene. Colleagues would gather around and thrust a pint into the officer's hand before requiring a blow-by-blow account. The cathartic interchange would most likely be accompanied by dark and inappropriate humour that any passing 'civvies' would be horrified to hear.

The Police Service had evolved since then, of course, now employing trained professionals to replace the alcohol-fuelled embraces and jokes, but Bare was sceptical that the outcomes were significantly better.

Whilst the decor and clientele of the pub had changed over the years the one constant that drew him back for an occasional drink were the couple who ran the place. Rona and Kevin looked the same to him as they had done when welcoming the rookie detective into their kingdom all those years ago. Each still occupied their own square yard of wooden floor at opposite ends of the bar, rarely chatting cordially to each other but always having a genuinely friendly greeting for their customers. Some regulars preferred the conspiratorial hushed discussions with Kevin, which normally ended in some clandestine deal. Back then no self-respecting detective would buy a new piece of electrical equipment without first checking whether Kevin could procure it at a discounted price first.

However, if it was innuendo-laden banter the customer required they would naturally gravitate toward the south end of the bar where the formidable Rona was in residence. Bare liked Rona, in fact he probably loved her in a way that he would be unable to explain to anyone else. At times she was a bawdy extrovert but was also at other times an equally adept quiet confidante with an uncanny knack of knowing which persona he needed. Over the years he had confided many a woe to her, rarely receiving any sage-like advice but always an attentive ear. Somehow this seemed to enable him to move from indecision to action without ever understanding how the process worked. Over the years it had also become a mutually understood ritual that Rona would critically appraise any new potential girlfriends. He smiled at the memory of introducing his late wife Julia to her. After only a few minutes Rona had pulled him to one side and told him to marry this one as he would never do any better. It of course came with the caveat that should Kevin meet an untimely demise she would claim Bare as her own.

"Well hello, stranger," she said, reaching across the bar and grabbing hold of Bare's tie. She pulled him toward her before planting a long kiss on his lips in the full gaze of her husband who was unperturbed, having witnessed the action countless times before.

"Rona, you look gorgeous as ever," said Bare when she allowed him to stop the kiss and straighten his tie.

"So why have you been ignoring us and staying away?" she said, accompanied with a comic pout of her artificially red lips unscathed from the kiss.

"Oh, you know, all work and no play," he replied with an apologetic shrug.

"Kevin said it was because you got promoted so now you can't mix with the rabble anymore," she said with an unnecessary gesture toward her husband.

"That's just wishful thinking on his part, he's worried one day we are going to run away together," replied Bare.

"Oh for God's sake don't tell him that. He would probably give us a lift just to get rid of me," she joked.

The ritual flirtation was interrupted by the arrival of Brady and he could tell from her demeanour she had news to tell him. After what seemed an unnecessarily lengthy greeting from Rona, Bare was gratified to find himself sitting opposite Brady in a quiet alcove.

"Any news about Amelia Hann?" he asked.

"No, nothing since we spoke but have you heard about Victor Kent?" she asked.

"What about him? He's an arsehole," replied Bare, struggling to hide his disappointment concerning the lack of an update on the missing journalist.

"He's been killed. There was a pile-up on the M12."

"Oh bloody hell," replied Bare as he sipped his drink and regretted his character assassination of the late ACC.

"It's a weird one, it looks like either he was trying to cross the road or it's suicide. His car was found in a lay-by on the A63 and he's walked through a wooded area to get to the motorway. I heard one of the traffic guys say his body stank of booze."

Bare had stopped listening to the description of the motorway accident and was remembering why he had grown to dislike the ACPO officer he had only met a few times.

"Kent did the foreword for Amelia Hann's book, he really bigged himself up. Avery would have hated him for that," he said.

He looked across at Brady, expecting to see confirmation of his evolving theory in her expression but instead just saw a confused response.

"Avery is dead, Seb, that's what I wanted to tell you, Hann's house is clean. I was wrong to call you, I think I overreacted. Besides, there is nothing to suggest anyone else was involved in Kent's death. You need to let it go," she implored and touched his hand to emphasise the fact that her words were designed to be supportive rather than critical.

"Sharon, you rang me because your gut reaction told you to. First Hann, now Kent. It's him, I'm telling you."

He didn't need to see a sympathetic smile on her face so stood up and hurriedly put his jacket back on.

"Seb, don't be like that. Come on, we can finish our drink and then talk," she implored.

"No, I need to go and speak to Woodham, Sharon. I know you don't believe me but please be careful, okay?"

She agreed that she would in an effort to placate him further but in an instant he was gone. She took a further sip of her drink whilst agonising over what to do next. Finally, she took her phone out of her bag and scrolled through her address book before selecting a name and initiating the call. The recipient quickly answered and Brady took a deep breath before speaking.

"Sorry to bother you, ma'am, it's Sharon Brady. You told me to keep you appraised about DI Bare and I thought I had better warn you he's on his way in to see you."

CHAPTER 28

The slow and methodical cleaning of the crime scene had done little reduce Sonia's accelerated heartbeat. She had doubted herself right up to the moment of Eve Kent's execution but now felt exhilarated at the memory. The actual murder, however, was almost an irrelevance, it was the look of approval he gave her that she would relive in her mind for the rest of her life. She knew now without hesitation that he was the one, her saviour and her future.

She wanted to feast on all his plans but had to content herself with the crumbs he was prepared to give her as they worked largely in silence. His consistent message was that the next few weeks were merely a bridge to a new life for them both. Sometimes when he described living with her abroad she would shut her eyes and try to visualise their paradise. She hoped he would allow her the autonomy of running their home, considering it to be an act of servitude. She of course wanted it to happen now but understood they were travelling at his pace and he needed closure before he could start a new life. It was vital to him that those who had wronged him were punished. She, of course, didn't know these people but nevertheless was learning to vicariously detest them for being his enemies.

When they had finished she helped him carry the plastic-sheet-wrapped body out to their car where it was placed in the boot. They then returned inside for one last check and he explained that despite all their work a police forensic team would have no difficulty in proving this had been the scene of a brutal murder. She had therefore wondered why they had gone to such lengths to clean it and he patiently explained it was that they had needed to remove the suspicion in anyone's mind that was necessary to pre-empt any further specialist investigation.

"It just looks now the same as when we found it, a long-term empty office unit waiting for a new company to occupy it. And one day some unknowing individual will work away doing their pointless job, oblivious to the fact this is the spot where you proved yourself," he said, gesturing to the now empty space on the floor.

"I will never let you down," she replied.

"And that's the reason I will always have you by my side and keep you safe," he said.

The deposition site for Eve was by a lake on their way home. The area was a beauty spot by day but in contrast the night made it an eerie and very lonely location. He positioned the body in such a way that it would appear to have been hidden by an amateur, a very shallow, hastily made grave with foliage as the main covering. Only when completed satisfied with his work did he add the finishing touch using the contents of the condom so diligently collected by Sonia.

The local radio news informed them that the motorway earlier closed in the wake of a fatal collision was now again open, so their journey home took less time than anticipated. Recognising it was getting late, they stopped to buy fish and chips and apologised to Mrs Warner for keeping her waiting for her evening meal. In truth she didn't mind at all and remarked it was nice to see the pair clearly enjoying each other's company.

After Sonia had left to go to her own home Avery retired to his bedroom and opened the packages that had arrived whilst they had been out. The array of covert surveillance equipment was inferior to that at the disposal of law enforcement agencies but was more than adequate for his purposes. More importantly, it was simplistic enough for Sonia to operate after appropriate instruction from himself, of course. Satisfied, he put the objects to one side and lay down on his bed. As soon as he closed his eyes he allowed himself to remember each delicious detail that had preceded the deaths of Victor and Eve Kent earlier that day.

CHAPTER 29

Much to his frustration Bare had been forced to wait until the following morning before gaining an audience with Superintendent Woodham. Once again she was the personification of calm, polite behaviour as she invited him in and ordered them both a coffee.

The delay had made Bare waver about vocalising his certainty that Avery had returned from the grave but nevertheless, he had decided to give it another go. This time he had vowed to himself to be more measured and had jotted down a number of bullet points on a sheet of paper to act as an aide-memoire. He had also exploited a long friendship with a Sergeant in the Traffic Department to learn more about Kent's death. By contrast Woodham had clearly decided it was not necessary to take notes on this occasion and her book used in their previous meeting, was nowhere to be seen. This irked Bare from the outset as he believed it to be an indication that she wasn't going to consider his thoughts with the gravitas they surely merited.

"So what can I do for you?" she asked unnecessarily, having been fully briefed by Brady the previous evening.

"I am just concerned that the possibility that Paul Avery is still alive is not even being considered especially after what happened to Victor Kent yesterday," he said.

"And what do you think happened to ACC Kent? I wasn't aware that the CIB now investigated Road Traffic Collisions," she replied, struggling to mask the irritation she was feeling.

"Well it's my understanding that there are a number of things that don't add up," replied Bare, unwilling to cite specifics and thereby expose his source.

"And any unanswered questions in the very early stages of an investigation automatically means we should focus on the ghost of Paul Avery? For goodness' sake, we are still trying to update all his family members about the poor man's death, Sebastian," said Woodham, pausing partly to sip her coffee but mostly to check her rising temper.

"Ma'am, I know you think it's a wild conspiracy theory but I can't get away from the facts. A journalist who wrote about Avery has vanished without a trace and a short time later the ACC who wrote a foreword in the same book and was Paul's line manager walks into traffic for no apparent reason. Avery is the common denominator." He emphasised his final point with a firm tap on the coffee table in front of him.

"Sebastian, there are lots of experienced cops working on both these cases, many of whom were here last year and remember only too well what Avery did to you and others. None of them seem to share your view that this demon you seem unable to exorcise is responsible. Now I am making allowances for you but this has to stop. You are not involved in these investigations and if any information was ever to come to light involving Avery you would never be allowed to be involved anyway. Are we clear?"

She only allowed him to sit in sullen silence for a few moments before she again checked the understanding of his position.

"Are we clear?" she repeated.

"Crystal, ma'am, and once again I apologise for voicing my concerns," he replied.

He stood up and walked toward the door, already thinking about his next move. In an effort to extinguish any residual flames, Woodham asked him to sit down a further time.

"This is not for wider circulation but he did have a reason," she said softly.

The confused expression on Bare's face made her realise she needed to clarify her statement.

"You said ACC Kent didn't have a reason to do what he did but there was a confidential briefing from the Chief this morning. Victor had been recently diagnosed with cancer, inoperable apparently. He was about to medically retire but had sworn the Chief to secrecy. We don't think he had even told his family. The Family Liaison Officers are walking around on tiptoes especially as his daughter has yet to be located and informed."

"Shit, so it could have been all too much for him," Bare said with a realisation that suicide was now much more plausible than he had considered.

"Exactly, but for your ears only," reminded Woodham.

Bare left her office and returned to his but upon noticing a cleaner polishing his desk turned on his heels and took a detour to Sharon Brady.

"How did it go with Woodham?" she asked.

"I don't think she is my biggest fan," he answered.

"Shocker, a woman not falling at Sebastian Bare's feet," teased Brady but averting any direct eye contact with him.

Bare took no notice of the comment and was clearly deep in thought. He was silent long enough for Brady to ask him if he was all right. Bare gave no answer as to the state of his health but responded with a question of his own.

"Sharon, what do you know about Victor Kent's daughter?"

CHAPTER 30

This time it was a far more confident Raymond Wilson who opened the door. He had even made the effort to comb his dark, greasy hair in anticipation of her second visit. The previous encounter had been relived a thousand times in his mind and he fantasised that the next would be even more erotic. Once again she looked unremarkable and her expression gave no hint as to her intentions but the recent memory had already made him aroused as he invited her in.

His ardour was, however, instantly dampened as he belatedly saw her colleague emerge from the exterior shadows and follow her into his flat. Sonia saw his obvious expression of disappointment and suppressed a smile as she introduced him to Detective Inspector Smith. She then motioned him to sit on the sofa and immediately sat alongside him whilst her colleague remained standing, casually surveying the hovel that Wilson called home.

"How have you been since I last saw you, Raymond?" she enquired.

"Fine," he mumbled, looking down at carpet submissively.

"Do you remember the last time I visited we spoke about my unconventional methods of rehabilitation?" she asked as he felt that familiar touch of her hand on his thigh.

He merely nodded in response, not willing to show anything other than minimal understanding in the presence of the unwelcome third party.

"Well this is phase two and I know how much you enjoyed phase one," she said, sliding her hand further along his thigh.

"What about him?" said Wilson, looking in the direction of Avery who was by now slowly wandering around the room casually examining random items as though browsing in a sub-standard antique shop.

"He's just here to make sure I do a good job," said Sonia, whose hand was now at his waistband, encouraging his trousers to once again come down.

Wilson instinctively knocked her hand away, unwilling to repeat the previous experience in the presence of Avery who had now moved behind the sofa. As yet, Wilson had not heard him speak but something about the man's demeanour made him increasingly menacing.

"In that case you're under arrest," said Sonia, producing some handcuffs from a pouch concealed inside her jacket.

"For what?" stammered an indignant Wilson as Avery roughly forced him to his feet.

"Just do as you are told," said Avery and Wilson felt the cuffs being applied behind his back by Sonia.

"I have done nothing wrong," complained Wilson. "You two are well out of order. I want to make a complaint."

Avery smiled before using a double-heel palm push into Wilson's chest, causing the handcuffed man to fall backward into a seated position on the sofa with his arms trapped behind him. The manoeuvre caused immediate pain to both his wrists due to his body weight falling onto the unforgiving steel bracelets he was wearing.

His cry of pain was stifled by the hand of Sonia across his mouth but was also quickly forgotten as he realised her free hand was now holding what appeared to be a very sharp hunting knife at his throat. His eyes darted back to her colleague and he was horrified to see that Avery was also now holding a similar knife that had presumably also been concealed about his person.

"Now listen, you little shit, I don't want to hear any complaints, in fact I don't want you to make a sound, okay?" said Avery as he towered over his seated prisoner.

Wilson rapidly blinked in acknowledgement, unwilling to risk any movement of his vocal cords in case that caused the knife held at his throat to move. Once satisfied he was compliant Sonia withdrew the knife before removing the scarf she had been wearing and quickly using it as a tight gag around him. His mind was racing as to what they intended to do to him but he had already decided he wasn't going to enjoy it as much as phase one.

Once satisfied that he was bound and gagged Avery nodded toward Sonia and from her standing position behind the sofa she placed a restraining hand on each of Wilson's shoulders. Wilson then saw his trousers being pulled down by Avery and the fear running through his body effectively paralysed him. He wasn't wearing any underwear in anticipation of another pleasurable encounter with Sonia so was fully exposed as his trousers reached his ankles and acted as an additional restraint. His state had moved beyond flaccid to almost full retreat into his body, causing Avery to laugh which added to the utter humiliation of his position.

Then to his horror he saw Avery again pick up the knife that had been carefully put to one side. He felt the grip of Avery's leather-gloved hand around his penis and his body tensed like it had never done before. Before he passed out due to the pain of his manhood being cut off he heard Avery say something about not moving in case it caused him to nick the femoral artery as well.

CHAPTER 31

Sharon Brady had been to countless crime scenes in her career but none had made her sadder. As she looked down at the lifeless body of the young girl she felt her professionalism start to dissolve. She despaired at seeing the aftermath of such a deliberate and cruel act perpetrated by another human being. Although no formal identification had been made it was obvious to her that she was looking at Eve Kent and she wondered how their family could cope with another agony message so soon after the last one.

She watched intently as the Crime Scene Investigators in their white overalls diligently performed their work. Each action was performed with meticulous care, as though they didn't wish to disturb Eve from her eternal slumber. Brady hoped that the killer's identity lay amongst the growing number of sealed exhibit bags but she didn't feel confident. If Bare was correct and Avery really was alive he was far too astute to give them a tangible clue. The thought of that man being alive sent a shudder down her spine and she chastised herself for allowing his image to creep into her mind.

She checked her watch and wondered when the Major Investigation Team would arrive and relieve her of the crime scene command. In normal circumstances the investigation of such a serious crime would be a reluctant baton to pass on. She, like many of her detective colleagues, considered murder investigations to be the pinnacle of their careers. But this felt different, too close to home and she knew herself too well to even pretend otherwise.

She had already been told that the Amelia Hann missing person enquiry would remain with her as there was insufficient evidence to suggest it could be linked in any way to the deaths of ACC Kent and his daughter. She was fine with that as it would necessitate regular contact with the MIT without being directly involved. She gazed down once again at Eve Kent and hoped that Amelia had not suffered a similar fate.

"You okay, Sharon?" asked the familiar figure of DCI Gareth Jones upon his arrival.

"Yes boss, it's a tight cordon so the CSIs are doing a thorough job," she replied.

"I didn't ask about the scene, I asked if you were all right," said Jones softly.

"In truth I'm not sure, this one has rocked me a bit," she replied.

She knew her admission would be treated in confidence by the senior detective whom she had grown to admire over the preceding twelve months. His reputation amongst colleagues was that of a rather dour and serious individual but she had found him to be a caring and compassionate man. He had been incredibly self-critical in the aftermath of last year's events but now appeared to have emerged as a better detective as a consequence. He also had taken on the role as an unofficial shoulder to cry on for affected colleagues and she had found that to be a rare but most welcome position.

"Do you think there is any chance...?" she asked without needing to finish the question.

"No, I don't think so," he replied, "but until what's left of his rotting remains wash up on some beach I will never discount it completely."

"You may get a visit from Seb Bare once he knows about this," she said.

Jones laughed and held up his phone so she could see the information displayed on the screen.

"Oh, just the seven missed calls," she noted.

"Just the seven ignored calls," corrected Jones.

CHAPTER 32

Avery quickly downloaded the footage from the covert recording devices he had equipped Sonia with the previous day. She had told him she had complied with his instructions but he reserved any praise until he had viewed the product. True to her word, he observed the video tour of the police station he knew so well and was pleased with the quality. She had entered as many areas as she possibly could have done without arousing suspicion and had provided slow panoramic coverage of all the briefing notes displayed. She of course had no real idea of the things that interested him the most so occasionally he would fast forward through the material. Sebastian Bare's office had yielded little in the way of information which he had found surprising. He remembered often chastising Sebastian for failing to adhere to the 'clear desk' policy and it was annoying that the officer belatedly now appeared to conform.

It was, however, the footage of the basement parking area that made Avery lean forward in his seat. Sonia had clearly spent a great deal of time recording footage of the various parked cars whilst putting rubbish in the nearby large bins. He had told her that staff habitually left their vehicles unlocked in the secure compound in case colleagues needed to move them. There were always more vehicles than official spaces, causing people to occasionally double park, inconsiderate of their colleagues' needs. He was excited to see that was one habit Bare had not changed as he carefully viewed the footage of the car's interior.

Sonia entered the room carrying his mug of coffee and made

some irrelevant remark about his surrogate mother who was asleep downstairs. He ignored the unwanted interruption before realising that an encouraging word was still a useful investment for him.

"This is really good work, Sonia," he said whilst still looking at the screen in front of him.

She made no response but he suspected she had blushed with gratitude at his praise. After spending another couple of minutes verifying the detail he needed he swivelled his chair in her direction.

"I need you to do something for me," he said, and saw she was already nodding in agreement to her unknown task. "I need you to go and buy two air fresheners, one that can be placed in an office and the other is for a car. The car one must be exactly the same as that," he said, pointing to the video image frozen on his screen.

She leaned forward and saw her task was to find a rather old-fashioned air freshener in the shape of some traffic lights. The liquid in the device was held where the amber light would sit. She recognised the product immediately and felt this was probably the least arduous thing he had asked of her to date.

"I know where I can buy one of those and as for the office, they supply us ones to place out at work, cheap white plastic things, would one of those be okay?" she asked.

"Yes, sounds perfect, you'll need to bring me one here," he said, and then turned his chair away again to signal that there was nothing else he needed to say.

She left the room and paused only briefly in the hallway downstairs to put on her coat. As an afterthought she entered the lounge to check on the sleeping Mrs Warner and softly covered the slumbering woman with a blanket across her legs. She was of course still the old lady's carer and saw no reason why she couldn't multitask this alongside her obligations to the serial killer sitting upstairs.

CHAPTER 33

Bare felt conflicted about the whistle-stop journey to Scotland. He of course wanted to see Cameron but also felt uneasy about the risk he was taking despite all the mitigation he had put in place. He could have imparted all his concerns over the phone but felt it important to present them in person. As she opened the door to greet him, Mary McKenzie immediately sensed that this unscheduled visit was also not purely a social one. Nevertheless, the pair engaged in small talk over dinner and took turns to quiz Cameron about his day at school before the boy unusually volunteered to retire early to his bedroom.

"So what's on your mind, Detective Inspector Bare?" she asked, handing him a generous glass of scotch.

"I'd better not drink all that, I'm driving back down tonight," he replied and then took a small sip of the excellent alcoholic beverage.

"Well it must be important for you to travel all this way for such a quick visit," she said, feeling increasingly uneasy about the conversation's direction of travel.

"Okay, a couple of things have happened which have made me suspect that Avery is still alive," he said, and this time took a larger gulp of his drink.

"You had better tell me everything then, Seb, and I mean every fucking detail," she commanded.

Bare went on to explain the disappearance of Amelia Hann, the strange death of Victor Kent and the murder of his daughter Eve. As he spoke aloud he again realised that the connections with Avery were tenuous and he braced himself for a disbelieving response. To his surprise, Mary McKenzie made no immediate comment but merely swirled the remaining liquid in her glass whilst she silently processed the information.

"I know I have nothing more than a feeling and it's probably my imagination running wild," said Bare to break the silence.

"Except I think you're right and I trust your instincts," she eventually replied. "So what do we do?"

Before he could answer, the dog that had been sleeping peacefully by the open fire sprang into life and ran barking toward the French doors that opened into the rear garden. Bare reacted immediately afterwards and told Mary to open the doors in thirty seconds and release the still barking Tyrus. He then made his way to the front door and waited for the sound of the running noisy dog to mask his own exit on the other side of the house. He quickly rounded the corner on the external side of the perimeter hedge and ran toward the spot he had examined on his previous visit.

As he did so he saw the dark silhouette of a figure running away across a field toward the road. Bare wanted to shout a command to stop but instead needed every ounce of his energy to maintain a sprint chase. To his frustration the distance between the pair was increasing and only adrenaline was fuelling his efforts to catch up. Then he saw the figure stumble over the uneven surface before falling to the ground. This provided Bare with his only opportunity to gain ground and from some forgotten reserves of energy he ran even faster. As his prey struggled to their feet Bare arrived and with a last-ditch rugby tackle hit the midriff of the other person. The impact caused both to fall to the ground but Bare was the quickest to react and he was able to land a punch somewhere that caused an exhalation of breath. This was the only encouragement Bare needed to launch a series of unreturned blows until he had control of the figure that he now saw was wearing a balaclava.

He was able to successfully employ his favourite arrest armlock and once satisfied it was in place he used his free hand to roughly remove the head covering. Even in the dim light afforded by the moon he could tell he had apprehended a much younger man. During the brief pursuit he had convinced himself he was chasing Avery and was disappointed that his prisoner was so clearly not his nemesis.

After regaining his breath he shouted at the young man.

"Who the fuck are you?"

A bright torch then shone on the pair and they were joined by Mary McKenzie and a snarling but thankfully leashed Tyrus. Mary directed the torch at the man's face, causing him to look away but not before she immediately recognised him.

"Let go of him, Seb, it's my nephew Patrick," she said in confused relief.

CHAPTER 34

As Bare drove back down the motorway he consoled himself with the fact that journeys in the early hours meant that traffic was mercifully light. He replayed the events of the previous night in his mind and wondered how the hastily convened McKenzie family conference was going. Patrick's revelation that members of the extended family regularly undertook surveillance at the property to safeguard Mary and Cameron had not gone down well with the former matriarchal lead of the Organised Crime Group. She had summoned her late husband's brother for an urgent meeting and Bare could not resist a smile as he imagined the man's trepidation.

He had offered to stay but considered her decision to dispatch him back south a wise one. He was confident that she would provide a plausible explanation for his visits without revealing the full extent of his relationship with Cameron, at least he hoped not. But most of all he derived some comfort from the fact that despite her 'retirement' it was clear there was still a layer of protection in place for Mary and her grandson.

Bare also felt vindicated that at least one other person now shared his belief that Avery was still alive. He hoped that in sharing his thoughts he had not fuelled an unnecessary paranoia that in turn would adversely affect Cameron, but justified that to himself as a proportionate risk. Whilst in that pragmatic mindset he had also made the call to Robin that he had been procrastinating over for days. He needed to keep her safe and if he was correct about Avery history told him anyone close would be very unsafe. He was also certain that had he revealed the true reason for keeping a safe distance apart she would have reacted defiantly. He therefore used the excuse of a heavy workload combined with unspecified feelings centred around 'moving too fast' to effectively hit the pause button on their relationship. She had appeared to reluctantly accept his request and her sad tone at the call's conclusion had made him feel bad.

Even though he was making good progress a check of the illuminated clock in the car made him realise he would not have time to go home before work. The prospect of a large but mundane workload on the back of a sleepless night did not enthuse him but it wasn't a unique occurrence. As he drove he felt himself reminiscing about some of the ridiculous stunts he had pulled over the years and miraculously avoided sanction. Inevitably this caused him to remember his late wife Julia and best friend Jim Morton. He missed them both and from nowhere felt a tear rolling down his cheek.

To avoid further self-reflection he pulled into the motorway services to refuel the hire vehicle and have his first coffee of what was likely to be many more that day. He calculated that even after dropping the car off and collecting his own he would still arrive at work earlier than most. He was therefore surprised when his phone rang and he saw that it was Sharon Brady calling him.

Upon answering the call Sharon immediately apologised to him, assuming she had acted as an unscheduled early morning alarm call.

"Actually I am already on my way in," he responded.

"Bloody hell, your new rank has really got you motivated," she teased.

"Well you know I like to lead by example. Anyway, what do you want, Sergeant?" he countered.

"Thought you might want to know there's been a development on the Eve Kent enquiry, fast-tracked lab result on some DNA and there is now a known suspect," she said.

"It's him, isn't it?" said Bare with absolute certainty in his voice.

"Behave, Seb. No, it's not him but it is someone you will know," said Brady, enjoying the power of her knowledge.

"Fuck's sake, Sharon, who is it then?" snapped Bare.

"You remember a sex offender you dealt with about ten years ago, Raymond Archibald Wilson?"

There was a prolonged silence as Bare tried to recall the man whose name was vaguely familiar.

"The seafront flasher!" prompted Brady.

The nickname that Bare himself had invented was all he needed to recall the serial sex pest who had threatened to singlehandedly destroy the town's tourist industry. Wilson had been so prolific at exposing himself to unsuspecting beachgoers that the enquiry had been escalated to a CID investigation and dumped from a strategic height onto Bare's desk. Nothing prioritised police enquiries quicker than an embarrassed mayor's wife who was in the same social clique as the Chief Constable.

"That can't be right, Sharon. Wilson was an insignificant little sex pest who literally wet himself when he got arrested," said Bare. "And in the back of my bloody car," came the indignant afterthought.

"Well, the MIT are mobilising an arrest team as we speak so they seem pretty certain. I will see you when you get in," said Brady.

Bare could tell that the way she terminated the call meant somebody had walked into her office so he resisted the temptation to call her back for further detail. He reflected on what she had told him and the revelation of a strong suspect made him doubt everything. If Wilson was indeed the man then it meant his trip to Scotland had been entirely without justification and his call to Robin unnecessary. Suddenly he became a lot keener to get to work.

CHAPTER 35

DCI Gareth Jones was not a fan of early starts but the adrenalin surging through his body meant he was wide awake. This was undoubtedly the highest profile case he had been involved in for over a year and he understood that politically it had to be perfect. The Constabulary needed this to restore public confidence and exorcise a few demons at the same time. Actually he needed this to silence some of the whispering critics that he suspected existed in every crowded room following his departure. To bring in a red-hot suspect linked to the murder of a colleague's daughter was the perfect retort to those who questioned his position.

As he received confirmation that all units were in position all eyes in the designated command vehicle turned to him. Like silent dogs straining at the leash they were anxious to be released. Any victim identified as being part of the police 'family' deserved additional effort on their part and each were secretly hoping that Wilson would not come quietly.

"Strike, strike, strike," was the simple command uttered by Jones into the radio causing each of the team to spring into action.

The covert, silent approach to the perimeter positions was replaced by a stampede of boots as the team rapidly approached Wilson's flat. They wasted no time at the front door, using the enforcer to smash the flimsy wooden obstacle open. The first officers inside had to step over the debris caused by their violent entry, each shouting, "Police!" by way of introduction.

Once Jones had been informed that the scene was secure he

quickly walked into the flat himself alongside Sharon Brady, who had been belatedly seconded onto the arrest team. They had only stepped a few paces into the flat when they were stopped by a uniformed Sergeant who had been the first through the door.

"You had better brace yourself, Guv'nor, it's not pretty in there."

Jones felt his heart sink instantly as this clearly was not going to be the straightforward arrest he had hoped for. The look on his experienced colleague's face made him gulp in nervous anticipation as he slowly walked further into the flat before he was in a position to fully survey what had been silently waiting for them.

Raymond Wilson was clearly not going to resist arrest, in fact Raymond Wilson was clearly not going to do anything other than continue sitting on his blood-soaked sofa. Jones slowly studied the dead man from a distance of about ten feet, glad that preservation of a potential crime scene meant he could not get closer. Despite the man's head being slumped to one side it was obviously Wilson, but identification was the only straightforward thing that Jones was trying to assimilate. The deceased man appeared to have his tracksuit bottoms around his ankles but there was so much blood it was difficult to make out for sure. Jones' gaze, however, was fixed on the seemingly obvious link between the large knife on the sofa and Wilson's almost severed penis that was still attached to the body by the slightest amount of remaining ligament.

Others in the room looked to Jones for some guidance but were apprehensive about disturbing the detective's train of thought. Sensing this, Sharon Brady barked a series of orders that invoked locking down the scene, summoning a senior crime scene investigator and controlling access to the whole building. As others responded to her requests she placed a gentle hand on Jones' elbow in an effort to break the trance he appeared to be in.

"Sir, is there anything else you need doing?" she asked.

"No, let's regroup back at the station," he eventually responded and the pair slowly started to leave.

As they walked carefully back toward the door Jones saw that a dining chair had been moved away from the table and its position in the room looked incongruous. He looked above the chair and saw that it appeared to be directly underneath the light fitting that was adorned with an old-fashioned upturned lampshade. Brady noticed him staring at the lampshade and was puzzled as to the attraction it obviously held.

"You got any gloves, Sharon?" he asked.

She was already wearing a pair of disposable ones but produced another pair from her pocket and unquestioningly passed them to him. He quickly put them on before standing on the chair and using the height advantage to reach up and feel inside the lampshade. After a couple of seconds he stepped down off the chair and she saw he had a small retrieved item in his hand. He passed her the small drawstring cloth bag he had collected and called across to a uniformed officer who was standing with a clipboard at the doorway.

"Can you mark that down as exhibit GJ/1?" he said and observed Brady place it into a small plastic bag which was duly annotated with the same reference number.

CHAPTER 36

The police station was eerily quiet when Bare arrived and the unusually empty car park provided an abundance of marked spaces. He chose an area where he was least likely to be blocked in and reversed into the allocated position. By the time he had completed the manoeuvre he saw that the electric gate at the entrance to the compound had closed with its customary efficiency. He retrieved his suit cover containing his office attire from the boot and quickly walked to the rear door which opened when he held his identification lanyard close to the sensor. Once inside instead of ascending the stairs in the direction of his office he took the opposite route to the basement locker room. After checking the wall-mounted clock, he assessed there was enough time for a much-needed shower before changing, although today would be a designer stubble look after he realised his razor was amongst the items still left in his car.

As the torrent of hot water hit his face he started to feel immediately refreshed after the long drive. He replayed the information in his mind that Sharon had provided him with earlier, hoping that the stimulus of water would help process it. It had been a number of years since he had encountered the man she had named as the prime suspect and he wondered what had happened to Wilson in that period. As he lathered the remnants of a discarded shampoo bottle into his scalp a grudging acceptance crept into his psyche. After all, if he couldn't spot a serial killer whilst working alongside him he could hardly claim with any certainty that the sex offender he had once dealt with was incapable of similar nefarious progression.

After switching off the shower he walked out of the cubicle, confident that at least one communal towel would be hanging in the tiled changing area for his use. Frustratingly, the only one he saw was a small hand towel that had seen many, many better days and he cursed his own lack of planning. With no other option other than using his own clothes he reluctantly took the towel off the metal hook and dabbed it across his naked body. It wasn't large enough to wrap around his waist so he merely draped it around his neck and walked to the peg where he had hung his suit, shirt and tie.

In his haste to regain the dignity of being once again clothed he turned a corner and literally bumped into the cleaner who shrieked with surprise. In one movement he pulled the towel from around his neck to his waist and held it firmly in place to prevent further exposure of his embarrassment. The pair then shared an awkward apology for being unaware of the other's presence in the room before they both hastily retreated in opposite directions.

As she left the locker room Sonia ascended the short flight of stairs to the ground floor just in time to witness a convoy of police vehicles drive into the car park. She then dutifully held open the rear door to allow the returning arrest team to file back into the police station. Occasionally one of the team acknowledged her act of kindness with a nod of gratitude but mostly she remained invisible to them. The last officer to walk through the door was a female who had paused to look at a familiar vehicle parked in the yard.

"Thank you, Sonia. I see DI Bare is in the building. Do you happen to know if he is in his office?" Brady enquired.

"No, he's in the locker room downstairs," she replied.

"Oh, thanks," said Brady, and the officer started to descend the stairs before Sonia grabbed her coat sleeve.

"You might want to give him a couple of minutes, he's, err, living up to his name at the moment," she said by way of explanation for her intervention.

CHAPTER 37

Brady's hesitation at the top of basement stairs had provided DCI Jones the opportunity to summons her to the Crime Scene Investigation offices and she could tell from his tone it was an impatient senior officer waiting for her arrival. The sterile surroundings and the attendance of the senior CSI allowed them to carefully inspect the exhibit seized by Jones at Wilson's home address. The nervous trepidation was palpable as the contents of the cloth bag were emptied onto the illuminated work surface to allow detailed inspection. The bag contained three items of jewellery – a gold ring, a silver charm bracelet and a delicate silver necklace.

The senior CSI methodically separated the items with a sterile tool that would have not looked out of place in a dental surgery. When each item occupied its own defined space on the work surface he studied them in turn with a handheld illuminated magnifying glass. Brady's attention, however, was focused solely on the necklace as the silver letter 'A' sparkled under the artificial light. She needed no corroboration but quickly began scrolling through the photographs on her phone so the others would accept her word. Finally she located the image of Amelia Hann that she had viewed a hundred times before when desperately seeking her whereabouts.

"That necklace belongs to Amelia Hann," she said whilst holding her phone for DCI Jones to view.

As he examined the image, she utilised the zoom function on the phone to eliminate any doubt in his mind that the necklace being worn by the smiling, carefree young woman was identical to the exhibit before him. He barely had time to digest the information when the CSI who had been examining the ring, added to it.

"The ring is inscribed, it has the name 'Eve'," he stated flatly.

"It was a gift for Eve Kent from her parents to mark her 18th birthday," added Jones, remembering the personal effects listed by the grieving Mrs Kent as being missing.

"I will get the items photographed and forensically examined," said the CSI, anxious to ensure that the integrity of the exhibits was retained.

"He was a fucking trophy collector, Sharon," said Jones, solemnly shaking his head at the futility of young innocent lives lost.

Brady nodded in agreement in the knowledge that the Hann missing person enquiry would now be upgraded to a murder investigation. She then turned her attention to the third item that had been in the bag. The charm bracelet was a pretty piece but it only had one small charm affixed to it. At first because of the design she had mistakenly thought it was an abstract bauble but when viewed from a different angle she could clearly see it represented a teddy bear.

"If Wilson only collected one trophy per victim we need to identify the owner of the bracelet as a priority," said Jones, reading the mind of his junior officer.

CHAPTER 38

It took less than 48 hours to fast track the priority exhibits recovered from Raymond Wilson's flat. The painful physical identification of Eve Kent and Amelia Hann's jewellery was supplemented by the discovery of additional DNA evidence which suggested the knife used by the man to castrate himself was the same weapon likely to have been used to cut Eve's throat.

Whilst the investigation remained fully staffed in an effort to locate the body of Amelia Hann and identify any other potential victims, the tension that had previously existed amongst senior officers had evaporated. Instead their energies were focused on the Media and Communications Department to ensure that all press interactions contained 'key messages'. The central theme of these were of course designed to subtly demonise the sex offender responsible for the atrocities whilst stressing how quick and efficient had been the police response. Previously invisible senior officers were now virtually clambering over each other to reassure the public that there was no ongoing threat whilst neatly side stepping any awkward references to previous events.

Avery enjoyed the unfolding theatre as he avidly watched each news channel in turn from the comfort of his own room. He took particular pleasure in the focused police efforts to locate the unknown owner of a charm bracelet that had been acquired for him by the dutiful Sonia. Initially the charm was going to be a ruby fish but he surmised that at least one of the dense detectives on the case would have hypothesised it was indeed a 'red herring'. So instead he had chosen the silver-haired bear as a homophone prophecy of his final victim.

He knew that Sonia was anxious for him to complete his work in order that they could begin his promised new life far away in the sun but he was not a man to be rushed. He was savouring each delicious chapter as the masterpiece he was authoring progressed. He of course knew the ending to his story but was struggling with some of the finer detail required to make it epic. He desperately wanted to engineer a situation where he could spend some precious time alone with Sebastian Bare. He wanted to see the expression on that man's face when he slowly began to understand how inferior his intellect was compared to that of his former boss. But most of all he wanted to see Bare's reaction upon the realisation his life would be imminently ending. He visualised an expression of abject fear but also considered there might be a flicker of futile defiance. He hoped the latter would be present as killing an angry person was somehow that little more exquisite.

His daydream was interrupted by a polite knock on the door and he realised it signalled the arrival home of Sonia. He made a mental note to afford her some specific praise as that seemed to generate a better work ethic. He remembered the various travel brochures that had arrived in the post earlier that day and quickly circled various random resorts with a marker pen before he permitted her entry.

"And how was your work today?" he asked after uncharacteristically greeting her with a prolonged tender embrace.

"It was good, I did everything you asked, all the things are exactly where you told me to put them."

"Oh, that's truly excellent work. I'm really pleased with everything you are doing, you're a superstar," he positively gushed.

"It was easy," she said, but her blush told him his compliments had caused the physiological reaction intended.

"Well ,you have one more task this evening. I've narrowed down some places we might set up home but would welcome your thoughts," he said, casually pointing to the pile of recently opened travel literature.

The haste in which she gathered the brochures betrayed her excitement and she was pleased he had already turned to face his computer screen and not witnessed it.

"But before you do that, I think Mother and I would welcome a cup of tea. I promised you would make one when you got in," he said casually, whilst tapping away on the keyboard.

"Right away, sir," she replied.

CHAPTER 39

Bare looked at the fully laden 'in-tray' which was a constant reminder as to where his attention ought to have been directed. He speculated whether he would feel better if he spent a few hours clearing it and concluded it would have a negligible effect on his mood. After a casual glance around he surreptitiously opened the larger of his desk drawers, knowing it was empty. The casual manoeuvre of transferring the paperwork to its new out-of-sight destination was much more satisfying than it ought to have been and he smiled inwardly in recognition of his occasional immaturity.

The clear desk signalled that he had earned a coffee and he ambled out of his office en route to the canteen. He was happy to make it a solo expedition, self-aware that his sullen mood would not make him good company. The route took him past the Major Incident Room which was normally crammed full with keyboard detectives but today it was deserted. He then remembered that DCI Jones was holding a meeting for all his staff elsewhere, a meeting that now held little interest for him, not that he had been invited in any case.

A young uniformed Constable stood outside the room and was peering inside in the hope of finding a detective. Bare sidestepped past him and hoped that the canteen would be equally devoid of people as the prospect of queuing for his coffee was not appealing.

"Excuse me, sir," called the Constable and Bare continued to walk away until he belatedly realised it was him being hailed.

He turned around and noticed that the officer was apologetically holding a piece of paper and clearly needed some assistance. He recognised the young man as being a relatively new arrival at the station and felt a wave of empathy about how bewildering everything was for new recruits.

"What can I do for you?" he asked.

"I was looking for one of the murder detectives but nobody seems to be about, it's just that I have a potential witness to the Eve Kent case at the front desk," explained the officer, relieved at being able to share his burden with someone senior to him.

"Well just record their details and tell them someone from the team will be in touch," replied Bare, secretly despairing at the lack of common sense on show.

"Yes, sir, it's just that the witness has just popped in on the way to the airport and they are disappearing for a few weeks on holiday so I didn't know if someone was available to quickly see them now?"

Bare felt slightly guilty about his initial judgement of the officer so offered to briefly speak to the witness to assess their value to the enquiry. He instructed the Constable to bring the witness to a nearby vacant interview room so a 'triage'-type interview could quickly be undertaken. As Bare waited in the room he contemplated whether it would be an abuse of his authority to dispatch the young officer to the canteen to collect his much-needed caffeine intake.

Within a few moments the officer reappeared at the door and Bare saw that he was now accompanied by two very senior citizens, each wheeling a fully laden suitcase in their wake.

"This is Mr and Mrs Thistlethwaite, they believe they saw Eve Kent shortly before she was, errr, went missing," announced the officer awkwardly.

"Please have a seat. I understand you are en route to the airport so hopefully we won't take up much of your time. I am Detective Inspector Bare. Perhaps you can explain what you may have witnessed?" said Bare.

Mrs Thistlethwaite was clearly the spokesperson of the pair and had barely sat down before commencing a detailed account of seeing all the news reports about the murders. As she detailed verbatim conversations between her and her husband, Bare sat with pen poised waiting to record something of interest in the space under where he had written their names. Finally she recounted a bus journey the pair had shared when they had seen a young woman they believed to be Eve Kent talking to a couple in the street.

Bare was not fully familiar with the finer detail of the case but he knew where the Kents lived and the type of car Eve possessed as that was still being sought. When both these details were mentioned in quick succession by Mrs Thistlethwaite he began making notes on the virgin piece of notepaper. She recounted how a professional-looking couple, both wearing facemasks, seemed to be having a detailed discussion with Eve Kent before all three had got into Kent's vehicle which had appeared odd.

"What do you mean by odd?" probed Bare.

It was then Mr Thistlethwaite spoke for the first time, causing Bare to contemporaneously record his exact words.

"It looked to me like the young girl had been arrested," he said.

CHAPTER 40

Superintendent Woodham briefly contemplated walking past the Major Incident Room without intervening but realised she had no choice given the number of banished officers standing in the corridor in an awkward silence. The sound of the argument within was escalating by the second and she recognised the voices of both the protagonists. Initially both men failed to notice her presence as she quietly entered the room and stood with her back against the door, arms folded. Finally she caught Gareth Jones' eye, causing him to stop mid-sentence. This in turn made Bare swing around with a short-lived intention to rebuke the person daring to interrupt the 'meeting'. Upon realising the identity of the visitor he, too, stopped speaking apart from a mumbled, "Ma'am," to acknowledge her presence.

"You do realise that you sound like hysterical schoolchildren in the playground?" came her rhetorical question.

The pair mumbled an apology and she struggled not to laugh at their sheepish expressions, using a brief nose scratch as a self-taught distraction technique.

"It was just a professional disagreement," offered Jones by way of explanation.

"Well it was clearly a disagreement so you're partially correct, Gareth," retorted Woodham, who was beginning to enjoy the obvious discomfort her entry had caused.

"Ma'am, some new evidence has come to light which throws the guilt of Raymond Wilson into considerable doubt," announced Bare to the obvious displeasure of Jones.

"Okay, let's hear it," she replied whilst simultaneously showing the palm of her hand to Jones to prevent his objection.

Bare was careful to relay his information in a calm, measured tone. He realised that Jones believed him to be overly emotive and was questioning his objectivity. Woodham listened quietly as he described the witness accounts of Mr and Mrs Thistlethwaite and why he considered them credible witnesses. DCI Jones also took the opportunity of his enforced silence to listen again to the much more rational Bare and found himself revising his opinion.

After answering a couple of her supplementary questions Bare waited to discover which side of the fence Woodham was going to position herself. Unexpectedly he received support from DCI Jones.

"Ma'am, I think that Seb has made some good points. We will of course generate some actions around this information."

Woodham was visibly pleased that calm had been restored but was keen to ensure her position was absolutely clear. Despite her many misgivings she knew that Bare was a good and intuitive detective but one that needed explicit instructions.

"Okay, to summarise, these new witnesses may or may not have witnessed the abduction of Eve Kent. From their descriptions it appears there were a male and female couple involved. We have no intelligence that links Raymond Wilson with a female accomplice and indeed their description of the male is not close to that of Wilson in terms of height and demeanour. That said, he remains our main suspect due to his antecedents and the overwhelming forensic evidence. I think you are right, Gareth, in that we need to T.I.E. this couple and then go from there."

Bare recognised that a commitment to trace/implicate or eliminate (T.I.E.) the couple was a positive step but found himself disappointed that Woodham had made no specific link between the manner of Eve's abduction and the modus operandi of Avery. He desperately wanted to raise the issue but could read her well enough to suggest it would only alienate someone he would later need in his corner. Any doubts he held as to her viewpoint were then quickly and unequivocally removed as she spoke once again.

"And Sebastian, I will remind you that this is a Major Investigation Team led enquiry and Gareth is the Senior Investigating Officer. There are no excuses for unprofessional approaches or off-the-books enquiries. I know he has an open mind to all possibilities but we follow the evidence, not any personal feelings or wild theories. I do hope we really understand each other."

"Perfectly, ma'am, although it's good to hear your reassurances about having an open mind," he replied in the knowledge this was the extent he could go without risk of sanction.

CHAPTER 41

Bare had no appetite to return to work so instead got into his car and waited for inspiration as to where to drive. Nowhere came immediately to mind so he sat in quiet contemplation. After a few minutes he began thinking about his late wife and moments later he realised why she had come into his mind. He imagined her sitting in the passenger seat and pulling a mad face in an effort to snap him out of his sullenness. The memory made him smile but more importantly he felt energised. The certainty of his plan swept through him like an adrenaline rush and he sprang out of the vehicle and rushed back into the police station. He was too pumped to wait for the lift so took the stairs, maintaining a swift pace until he reached his office. After closing the door behind him he reached for his desk phone but then hesitated before replacing the receiver without making the call he had intended. Instead he took a moment to sit at his desk and gently massage his temple with rotating fingertips. This was a habit he had developed since childhood and seemed to help his concentration and alleviate stress.

The meditation made her entry into his office go unnoticed so she made an exaggerated comic cough to gain his attention. He looked startled at first but then smiled at the manner of her intervention.

"I got your text. What's so urgent?" asked Brady.

"I need to tell you something. Can we got for a drink?" he replied.

"Do you use that line on all your women?" she teased.

His raised eyebrows indicated there was little appetite for their normal banter so she merely said, "Sure, let's go," and he quickly followed her out of the office. He told his deputy he was visiting his 'other' office should he be urgently required on the way out. He and Brady then shared a lift ride to the basement with a support staff member neither really knew so conversation was minimal.

Brady's question regarding which vehicle they should take was answered by Bare striding toward his car and gallantly opening the passenger door for her. Once inside he didn't immediately start the engine but turned slightly sideways on his seat to face her.

"Sharon, there is something I should have told you a long time ago," he began.

"Now you have me ever so slightly worried," she said in an effort to diffuse the rapidly growing tension between them.

"You remember the boy last year, Cameron McKenzie and everything that happened?" he continued. He was speaking very slowly, almost in the hope she would complete his sentences but in truth she had no clue as to the direction of travel of the conversation so she just nodded.

"I found out after Julia's murder that Cameron is my son. Nobody knows except his grandmother, not even the boy himself," blurted Bare.

Brady's jaw dropped in astonishment as she struggled to comprehend what was being said.

"Fuckity fuck fuck," she eventually exclaimed.

"Yep, that's pretty much what I said at the time I was told," replied Bare.

"You were sleeping with Liam McKenzie's wife? What the fuck were you thinking, Seb? Is that why that family hated you so much?" she shouted, the growing anger evident in her eyes.

"No, it wasn't like that. I was running Shannon as an informant, she came to me for help as Liam was abusing her, it was a one-time thing, a big mistake on my part."

"It wasn't a mistake, Seb, you took advantage of a vulnerable woman and exploited her as much as her husband," she said.

Bare felt wounded by the accusation and although he could have offered mitigation he chose not to as he knew deep down she was right. Instead he provided more detail about his history with the McKenzie family.

"Shannon told me the information about the robbery the McKenzie brothers were planning and I used it to be in the right place at the right time to arrest them. Getting Liam locked up was the best I could do for her. I never knew that Cameron was mine until Mary McKenzie told me," he explained.

He used her nonverbal communication as a cue to continue the story, explaining how he and Mary McKenzie had a mutual desire to track down the killer who had personally affected them both. He admitted that that he had continued to occasionally visit Cameron post-Avery and that he had developed feelings for his son but in truth had no idea where it would lead.

Brady remained silent. Occasionally her displeasure surfaced with a slow shake of the head but for the most part she tried to remain impassive. Once again this man was provoking feelings that she hoped were no longer there and this time it was an irrational sense of betrayal that was hurting her the most. Only when she felt able to control herself did she finally speak.

"Why are you telling me all this now, Seb?" she asked with genuine wonder.

"Because if Avery is still out there I know he'll come for me and I need someone I trust to look out for Cameron. He has already tried to kill him once. If he ever found out he was my son..."

"Fine, thanks for the burden," she replied with no attempt to disguise the bitterness in her tone.

"For the most part he is well protected by family and obviously miles away from here, but I have told his school that if you ever contact them they can trust you implicitly. Anyone else and they will instigate an emergency protocol I have set up. It's called Operation Stockmarket," he explained.

"Sounds like you've got it all sorted. Guess you knew I would help before you asked me," she replied.

"I know it's a lot to ask but you're the one person left that I truly trust, Sharon. I will tell you the details on the way to the pub. I think we both need that drink now," he said and finally started the car engine.

CHAPTER 42

As the rain lashed down she regretted not phoning ahead to tell him she was coming. Another impatient press of the door buzzer still yielded no response so reluctantly she took out her phone and tried to call him. He could hardly make an excuse not to see her as she had travelled all the way from London, she decided. His phone diverted straight to voicemail and she briefly considered leaving a message but instead took the opportunity to flag down a passing taxi that mercifully stopped.

"I'm not supposed to pick up fares but you look like you were getting drenched," greeted the driver.

"Thanks, you're a life saver. Can you take me to the police station?" asked Robin.

The fifteen-minute journey was mostly in silence, occasionally punctuated with references to the weather and criticism of other road users by the driver. Robin took little notice and instead used the time to reflect on her spontaneous decision to visit Bare despite him telling her explicitly not to. Her motivation had been a combination of disappointment and confusion. She of course understood his wish to take things slowly but had felt there had been a growing connection between them over the recent months. Then she had received the phone call where he had been evasive and distant. She sensed he was not telling her everything and felt compelled to act. Her past was littered with relationships that ended badly and she needed to know if this was heading in the same direction. She felt strongly that he at least owed her that.

After paying the fare she quickly entered the police station. It was an old-fashioned building compared to the premises where she worked in London but she liked the traditional wall-mounted blue lamp by the entrance. She had been a regular visitor there during the official enquiry when she had provided detailed accounts of how she had grown to suspect her former boss due to irregularities on an exhibit sheet. She was thankful that the station clerk on duty was the one she was most familiar with, which negated the need for introductions and explanations. Instead she was merely buzzed into the inner sanctum with an accompanying cheery wave.

She made her way to the lift and wondered how Bare would receive the visit. It then occurred to her that he might not even be at work and the foolishness of her journey would be amplified further. As she walked toward his office the signs were not promising as it appeared dark and unoccupied. Her heart sank as she got closer and her initial observations were confirmed. His washed coffee mug upturned on the desk indicated Bare had probably left for the day and she turned on her heels to retrace hep steps toward the lift. A man she vaguely recognised as his deputy noticed her presence and intercepted her journey.

"Hi, he's at his other office," said the man whose name she was embarrassed to have forgot.

"Oh right, thanks, I only popped in on the off chance of catching him. I didn't realise he had another office to be honest," she said awkwardly.

"No, that's just the code name for the Swan. You only missed him by half an hour so he should still be there," he said in a manner that suggested she ought to know where the pub was located.

"Oh, thanks, that's brilliant. Nice to see you again," she said quickly before departing in an equally hasty manner.

A more detailed enquiry with her station clerk friend before leaving the building suggested the Swan Public House was either a very short drive or a medium-length walk away. As it had stopped raining she chose the latter rather than wait for a local taxi. She felt that an unannounced interruption of a Bare 'social' was justified given the miles she had travelled but remained unsure as to how it would be received. He had never taken her to this establishment or even mentioned it which she felt was strange given the obvious familiarity it held for him.

Inside the Swan Bare patiently waited at the bar to order the second round of drinks. He was in no particular hurry to return to the table where Brady sat quietly and deep in thought. Oblivious to the intensity of their discussions that followed their arrival at the pub, the landlady teased Bare about his 'date'.

"Nice to see you lovebirds back together after all this time," laughed Rona, nodding toward the waiting Brady.

"You couldn't be more wrong," Bare said after taking a sip of the double scotch he had ordered as a 'chaser' to his pint of lager.

"Oh dear. Don't tell me your love life is still tangled. I told you we should just elope," she said and playfully grabbed his tie and pulled him close enough to kiss.

The moment was perfectly timed to coincide with Robin's entrance and she witnessed first the kiss and then Bare's walk back to the table he was sharing with Sharon Brady. Although he had only ever referred to her in a work context she had suspected the pair shared a history. As she witnessed Bare tenderly touch Brady's shoulder after placing the drinks on the table she felt her suspicions were entirely valid. Fuelled by a jealous adrenaline she marched up to their table and without saying a word emptied Bare's partially consumed beer over his head. The previously noisy pub became suddenly quiet as Robin turned and walked to the exit with her head held defiantly high as the silence turned to a loud cheer from the regulars, delighted at the unexpected entertainment.

CHAPTER 43

Avery listened to the recording for the seventh time in succession as he sat in his car opposite the Swan Public House. He had been patiently waiting for Sonia to finish work and had parked a safe distance away from the police station when he had received the activity notification from the covert recording device in Bare's car. The first time he listened the noise from passing traffic made him think he had misheard so he quickly replayed the recording. The excitement of its content made him play an imaginary drum on his lap before he quickly desisted the action in case it drew unwanted attention from passing pedestrians. Realising the pair were en route to the pub he had quickly called Sonia and told her to catch the bus instead. This was going to be a rare opportunity to surveil his prey and he was anxious to observe whether Brady was as angry as she had sounded. To his annoyance the one-way system in operation meant he arrived at the pub after them, as a drive-by confirmed Bare's vehicle was already in the car park. Luckily the on-street parking opposite gave him an ideal vantage point and he rationalised that the risk of compromise was small. He settled down to wait for their exit and was grateful that the fading light aided his camouflaged position.

He was prepared to wait a very long time as he had lots of thinking to do in light of the new-found information. He realised now that fate had provided him the perfect opportunity to create the theatre he craved that would immediately precede the death of Sebastian Bare. A number of hastily constructed scenarios were played in his mind before each in turn was discarded to make way for a new, improved version. The meticulous planning necessary for a perfect execution made him almost giddy with excitement. The distraction of his imagination made him miss Robin's entry into the licensed premises but he could scarcely miss her melodramatic exit a few moments later.

Any doubts as to the identity of his former analyst were removed as she was quickly joined outside by a very wet-looking, agitated Bare. The pair appeared to be having a heated argument but Avery was frustrated that he was too far away to hear the content of their animated exchanges. It appeared at one point that Bare was attempting to calm the situation and was cajoling Robin into returning inside. He could, however, tell from her body language this was an unlikely outcome as she seemed intent on walking away. Bare then seemed to motion toward his car as an alternate proposition and this seemed to gain more traction as the pair started to walk together in that direction. Almost comically it was obviously evident that Bare was then unable to unlock his car having left his keys inside. He rushed back into the pub and Avery saw Robin momentarily hesitate before walking off, having apparently decided not to wait.

Having retrieved his jacket and car keys Bare made a rushed apology to Brady who graciously encouraged him to "go sort things out with Robin".

"Do you need a lift, Sharon?" he asked out of courtesy, fervently hoping she would decline.

"No, I think that would be unwise, don't you, Sebastian?"

"Okay, thanks," said Bare and quickly made his way outside.

There was no sign of Robin where he had left her and no clues as to which direction she had walked away. Bare looked skyward for some divine inspiration but only saw the foggy night sky which perfectly matched his thoughts. He rationalised that she was probably making for the train station so unlocked his car and quickly headed in that direction.

Avery struggled to interpret what he had witnessed but knew for certain that Bare and Robin had left the pub in completely opposite directions. He assumed that Brady had remained inside or left prior to his arrival so was faced with a decision as to what to do next. The curiosity about Robin's unexpected appearance became the deciding factor and he pulled away slowly from the sanctuary of his parking spot to see if he could find her. Curiously she had appeared to walk off in the direction of an industrial site and he struggled to imagine what her intent there could be.

In truth Robin's only intent was to seek solace in her own company whilst walking in the general direction of what she mistakenly believed to be the next train home. The anger had dissipated and had been replaced by a malaise of disappointment. She blamed Bare for, well, being Bare, but most of all she blamed herself. Her sixth sense had been screaming when he had made the call to 'slow things down' but she had foolishly ignored it. Instead she had sacrificed her dignity in front of a pub full of strangers and Sharon bloody Brady who clearly possessed something she did not. She inserted her ear buds so that the music would drown out her own thoughts and strode purposefully in the wrong direction.

CHAPTER 44

This was not part of the plan, thought Avery as he spied the lone female walking steadily away from the lights of civilisation. He knew that he should turn around and go home; everything he wanted was suddenly in reach and attainable, yet here he was, stalking. Perhaps the instincts of a voracious hunter were too strong to resist, he mused. His heartbeat was accelerating as he visualised his gloved hand reaching around from behind and pulling her by the neck to an out-of-sight place. Her eyes would flicker with terrified recognition just before he killed her and he knew it would be delicious.

Then the other voice in his head spoke, reminding him this would merely be a quick fix and the effects would be transient and ultimately disappointing. But most importantly any spontaneous action would jeopardise everything. After all, he had promised himself that self-discipline was his most important ally.

Now he was out of his car, walking on the opposite side of the road but remaining behind her peripheral vision. He was taking care to walk with soft footsteps as his thoughts continued their internal argument. He knew himself too well; once the foreplay had started it became increasingly difficult to stop and he was fast reaching the point of no return.

She stopped at a junction, hesitant about her route and he saw the illumination of her mobile phone as she tapped the map application for guidance. He took refuge in the recess of a bus shelter and watched her shake her head slowly before turning around and walking back in his direction. Having already walked the route he knew that she would soon be back in a more populated area. Unwittingly, she was forcing him to make a decision.

With her music close to full volume she didn't hear the approach. The first indication of his presence was the touch on her shoulder and she let out a frightened squeal before turning to face him. He was saying something but the music drowned out his speech so she removed the ear buds.

"I said, you're walking in the wrong direction," said Bare.

He opened the passenger door of his car and she got in without comment as he walked around to the driver's side.

"So do you want to go to the station or back to mine so we can have a chat once I have got changed out of my beer-soaked shirt?" he asked.

"Yours," she said flatly before replacing the music in her ears.

Avery watched the car pull away and mouthed a silent 'thank you' to Bare. Only when satisfied the car was out of sight did he emerge from the bus shelter and walk back to his own parked vehicle. It had been an interesting evening in more ways than one and he was thankful that his own indecision had probably saved him.

When he arrived home Sonia was in the process of serving dinner to his 'mother' and both appeared genuinely pleased to see him. He declined the offer of a meal and went upstairs to his room in the knowledge that Sonia would soon follow with his coffee. When she arrived he asked for her warrant card as he had to make some adjustments to it. She dutifully handed it over without question and stood by his side as though waiting for further instruction.

"You remember what DS Sharon Brady looks like?" he asked.

"Yes, I've met her a couple of times," she replied.

"Good. I need you to go online and buy a wig, as close to her hairstyle and colour as you can find. You need to have it as soon as possible," he said and once more swivelled his chair around to face the computer screen which signalled the end of the conversation.

CHAPTER 45

Bare emerged from the bathroom in more casual attire, his hair still wet from the shower. He saw that Robin had opened some wine and poured them both a glass which he hoped would be for consumption rather than eveningwear. She was standing at the window looking at the red and white lights of the traffic below and did not appear to notice his presence. Normally he would have enveloped her with an embrace, maybe a tender kiss on the neck but instead he merely thanked her for the wine.

"I'm really sorry about the pub. I don't know what came over me," she said.

"I know exactly what came over me, knew I should have stuck to spirits," replied Bare and they both laughed.

During the conversation that followed Bare emphasised that Brady was not a love rival and that the pair were just mates and work colleagues. Whenever the talk risked getting too serious he teased her by saying he could not give the same assurances about the landlady and fully anticipated that one day they would indeed elope together. Robin laughed at his silly and irreverent sense of humour but was astute enough to know that its primary purpose was that of a defence mechanism.

For a brief moment Bare considered telling her the whole truth about Cameron but then stopped himself in the hope that there would be a more appropriate time and place to detonate that particular bomb in the future. Instead he provided some explanation about his desire to slow down their relationship by voicing his concerns about Avery.

She listened intently both from a personal and professional perspective. With her background as a crime analyst she was used to piecing together seemingly unconnected fragments of information to make a picture. He didn't reveal everything he knew or suspected as he genuinely didn't wish to alarm her but gave her the context he could tell she needed to hear.

"So in summary, you are just being my knight in shining armour and keeping me at arm's length for my own protection until you have slayed the nasty dragon?" she teased.

"And they say your degree in psychiatry is wasted," retorted Bare.

"No, they say my degree in philosophy is wasted," corrected Robin with a wine-induced giggle.

"Okay, I stand corrected," said Bare, topping up her half-full glass.

"But I have identified a major flaw in your otherwise cunning plan, Mr Knight," she said whilst wagging a reproachful finger in his direction.

"And what would that be?" asked Bare, enjoying the company of the now carefree, attractive younger woman.

"Dragons are not real things, they're just figments of your imagination, so can we please just go to bed now?"

Bare smiled and picked her up off the sofa, causing her to laugh even more as he struggled to carry her to the bedroom.

"Tell that to all the people who get burned alive," he mumbled but his words were lost in her continued laughter.

CHAPTER 46

After taking Robin to the station and insisting he wait until he saw her train depart, Bare arrived at work ten minutes late. After being briefed by his deputy he hurriedly joined the conference call held every morning to update senior officers on overnight events. The meeting was colloquially known as 'morning prayers' and ensured everyone was up to date on local policing initiatives and events. Bare contributed little to the meeting but listened intently as his peers took their turn to update senior officers. He was disappointed that DCI Jones made no mention of any progress in the murder investigations and the general contentment expressed by others about the way the enquiry was progressing.

After the meeting concluded he sought out Brady and eventually found her sitting alone in the canteen. After treating himself to a 'hangover cure' fried breakfast he sat opposite her and didn't object when she stole a piece of his toast from a side plate.

"I take it you managed to get things sorted with Robin last night?" she asked.

"Yes, sorry about that. I've just dropped her off at the station. She sends her apologies to you too," said Bare.

"No need to apologise to me, I wasn't the one who got wet," smiled Brady.

"I think she misinterpreted what she saw," explained Bare.

"Which bit? You snogging Rona or having an intimate drink with your ex?" asked Brady in as casual a tone as she could manage.

"Erm, probably you more than Rona. I think she perceived you as a bit of a threat," explained Bare.

"Oh, great, another Sebastian Bare worry to add to my growing list," said Brady, taking the opportunity to take the last remaining slice of toast left on Bare's plate.

"Yeah, well, we didn't really get a chance to discuss that other worry before we got interrupted last night," said Bare. He paused eating his breakfast to try and gauge something from Brady's expression.

"Don't worry, I thought about it last night. Your secret is safe with me, Daddy," came the barbed reply.

"It's more than a secret though, Sharon. I need a promise that if anything happens you'll look out for him," said Bare, emphasising the request he had made the previous evening.

"And I said I would," promised Brady, briefly touching his hand to signify it was a binding contract.

Bare exhaled and pushed aside his half-finished meal. His appetite had diminished due to thoughts swirling in his head.

"Good. I just needed to know that as I think things could soon happen," he said in a hushed, almost conspiratorial tone.

"What are you talking about, Seb?" she said, leaning forward in the expectation he would expand on his previous statement.

Before he could speak they were joined by Gareth Jones who having entered the canteen made straight for them rather than join the coffee queue.

"Jehovah's Witnesses," announced Jones, leaving Bare and Brady looking at each other in a confused state.

"Come again, boss?" said Bare.

"Jehovah's Witnesses," repeated Jones, expecting them to gain a new understanding of his repeated words. Upon realising there was no such understanding evident he explained further. "House-to-house in the street where your pair saw Eve Kent has revealed a number of houses got visits that day from a smartly dressed man and woman. Bloody Jehovah's Witnesses! Case closed," he said triumphantly.

"But that makes no sense. Why would Eve Kent get in a car with a pair of Jehovah's Witnesses?" replied Bare dismissively.

"I don't know, lad. God works in mysterious ways! But it's more logical than any of your theories," smiled Jones who immediately turned away, having spotted an opportunity to queue jump for his much-needed coffee.

CHAPTER 47

Avery had not slept for nearly twenty-four hours but was far from tired. His broad plan had been refined a thousand times in his mind and now he was concentrating on the finer detail. He tested the theory by imagining a barrister standing in the corner of his room firing a series of hypothetical questions at him. Only when he had exhausted all the 'what if' questions would he allow himself the freedom to move on. He knew that working alongside someone brought a whole set of new variables into play but he was confident she was ready. When it was all over he planned to feast on the memories for the rest of his life.

Finances were starting to become an issue and he was frustrated that there had been no early offers on Sonia's property that had gone on the market the previous week. He made a mental note to instruct her to chase the Estate Agents tasked with the sale. The proceeds of that together with his own inheritance would provide a comfortable if not lavish lifestyle for him in the future. The bonus of once again living alone would be priceless irrespective of where his new home was.

At that point his thoughts began to drift and he recognised that perhaps he did need some sleep after all. He figured that another hour finalising details and making the arrangements online would make the sleep that followed more restful. With a deep breath to aid his resolve he began searching the internet. His first task was to find a remote holiday home within ten miles of the area he had highlighted on a map in front of him. It proved to be a much easier task than he had anticipated as everything in that area appeared to be remote. The lifting of many of the pandemic restrictions meant there was wide availability too so he was spoiled for choice. After perusing numerous properties he settled on one that met all his criteria and completed the booking in the name of Linda Warner, using her debit card to pay in full. He had assumed full control of the woman's finances so there was no risk of her seeing the booking on a bank statement.

The act of depressing the button on the keyboard which confirmed the booking signalled his commitment to the challenging self-imposed timescale. Experience had told him that opportunities could never be taken for granted in this fluid world and the risk of delay was significant.

His imaginary barrister was now asking him what would happen if there was another lockdown? What would happen if restrictions around travel to holiday homes were re-introduced? What would happen if schools were once again closed?

His answer was that whilst he acknowledged the risk, there was no indication on the news that any of these things were likely to happen and certainly not within the next six days. He visualised the learned counsel acknowledging how compelling Avery's testimony was and this in turn permitted him to sleep.

Sonia entered the room about thirty minutes later and found him in the foetal position on his bed. She quietly covered him with a blanket and turned down the volume of the local radio channel he insisted on listening to throughout the day. She had contemplated turning it off but assumed that would most likely annoy him when he awoke.

She then retrieved his empty mug from the computer desk and looked around for any other tasks she ought to undertake. The waste paper bin appeared empty and nothing else suggested she had more work to do. As she was about to leave she noticed a single sheet of printed paper in the printer tray. As it was face up she was able to read it without fear of snooping so her curiosity made her scan the document with a casual glance.

She then left the room and quietly closed the door behind her. As she walked down the stairs she wondered why the increasingly frail Mrs Warner would want to go on a mini break to Scotland.

CHAPTER 48

Bare perused the confidential daily intelligence sheets he had received from the Dedicated Source Handling Unit. His role was to act as a conduit between the covert unit that ran police informants and the proactive units that acted upon the intelligence received. In essence he 'quality assured' the intelligence and decided which bits were worthy of a policing response. It was a common frustration that there were not enough resources to act upon all the intelligence received so he had to be selective. The Constabulary had published 'performance targets' it was striving to attain so the information that supported those areas was normally treated as a priority. Bare's scrutiny of the documents allowed him to add a couple of other priorities. Of course anything remotely linked to a possible sighting of Avery was immediately actioned but these tended to be rare and erroneous. His other area of particular interest was any reference to the McKenzie Organised Crime Group.

Since her 'retirement' and relocation to Scotland Mary had assured him that her family were no longer criminally active in the area. He replayed her assurances in his mind as he studied the intelligence report in front of him. He then picked up his phone and called his counterpart who was in charge of the DSHU. After the normal pleasantries had been exchanged he cut straight to the point.

"The informant who gave the intel about the McKenzies being back in town, are they reliable?" he asked.

"We don't have informants anymore," replied Detective Inspector Jed Chase.

"Okay, the Covert Human Intelligence Source," replied Bare wearily.

"If you look in the top right-hand corner of the form you will see a thing called the intelligence grading," said Chase.

"For fuck's sake, Jed, I've seen how you have graded it, I just want to know if they are solid, 'cause this is the first time since I've been in the chair that I've seen any reference to the McKenzies," snapped Bare.

"Sorry, mate," said Chase after belatedly remembering Bare's connections to the OCG. "Yes, solid as a rock. That particular CHIS has never let us down."

"Cheers, Jed, sorry about that. Can you task them to dig a bit deeper as to what's going on?" Bare requested in a moderated tone.

"Already done it, mate. So how you enjoying your new role? I would quite fancy that in my lead-up to retirement," half-joked Chase.

"Well anytime you fancy a job swap just let me know, it's not very exciting," Bare said wearily.

After replacing the receiver Bare considered what Chase had told him. He liked the man and more importantly trusted his professional judgement. He placed the intelligence sheet containing the information into his desk drawer and locked it. If Jed Chase said the informant was reliable then they almost certainly were. Then he put on his jacket and left his office, telling a staff member he was walking into town for a sandwich. Having walked away from the police station he used his private mobile to call the number he now knew off by heart. It was answered almost immediately.

"Some of your family have been seen in town. Anything I need to know about?" he asked.

"Still got your network of spies active then, Sebastian," said Mary McKenzie.

"I thought we had an understanding," said Bare.

"We do, darling, don't worry, they're just down there to collect the last payments owed from the people who bought our business. You wouldn't want my pension pot reduced, would you?"

"How long are they going to be in town?" he said curtly.

"I would imagine it will only take a few days, darling. I'll tell them to keep a low profile," she replied, pre-empting his request.

"Thanks. How's Cam?" he asked in a softer voice.

"He's good, he will be home from school at 4 o'clock if you want to speak to him?" she said and he recognised the genuine consideration in her voice.

"No, it's okay, I'll be working till late," he replied before terminating the call.

CHAPTER 49

"So, any questions?" he asked.

They had been repeatedly over the plan for the last few days in detail to the point where she literally could not think of anything else to ask. She silently shook her head before exhaling a long breath in the hope it would calm her rapidly beating heart.

"I have never relied on somebody else to do something this important before," he said truthfully, "but I have complete faith in you."

His added assurance was all she needed to hear and she smiled broadly. She had never felt more alive or confident. She knew that all she had to do was play her part and then they could move on to the next chapter. She could almost taste her new life and knew it would be delicious.

Avery carried the small suitcase down the stairs despite her insistence that she could manage and bade Mrs Warner a fond farewell. The woman looked at her with a confused expression that invited an explanation from Sonia.

"Remember, I said I was going on a short holiday and will see you when I get back. Don't worry, Michael will be here to look after you," Sonia said slowly.

"Where are you going, dear?" said the woman, increasingly frustrated that her thoughts had become more muddled in recent weeks.

"She's going on a bear hunt, she's going to catch a big one," interjected Avery, causing the woman to finish the children's story herself.

"What a beautiful day, we're not scared," sang the woman with her arms aloft. "I used to read that story to my son when he was young. Where is Michael?"

"I'm right here for you, Mother," said Avery, taking a gentle hold of the woman's still outstretched hand.

After reassuring Mrs Warner she would be back soon Sonia made her way to the front door. Avery hugged her and instructed her to 'be safe' before handing her the altered warrant card in its black leather folder.

"There you go, DS Brady, you'll be needing this," he said before closing the front door quietly behind her and returning to the lounge.

He poured the woman a small glass of water and handed it to her together with some tablets.

"Time for your pills, Mother," he said.

"I think I have already taken them today," she said, staring at the medication as it rested in the palm of her hand.

"Yes, that was this morning, don't you remember the doctors have increased your dose, Mother?" said Avery.

"Oh, did they? To be honest I can't remember," she replied before putting the tablets in her mouth and washing them down with a gulp of water.

"Thank you, Michael. I don't know what I would do without you," she added.

"Well, you can repay me by putting the kettle on," he said, helping the woman to her feet.

CHAPTER 50

Bare had worked late, partly because his neglected workload had been screaming for attention but mostly because he was in no hurry to return to his empty home. During the latter part of his marriage he had often craved the freedom of solitude but now felt he was overdosing on it. Almost reluctantly he walked toward the exit, drawing little satisfaction from his unusually clear desk behind him, and contemplated whether to make a visit to his favourite pub. He had not returned to the Swan since the incident with Robin and knew he would be ribbed without mercy by the regular punters, but that was still the better option than home.

When the lift doors opened he saw that Gareth Jones and Sharon Brady were also apparently heading out of the police station. He stepped into the lift to join them and despite their assurances to the contrary felt like he was interrupting a conversation between them. Jones was quick to start a fresh conversation and Bare knew it was a tactic to prevent him asking about the murder investigations. He played along as he was not really in the mood for confrontation in any case.

When the doors opened on the ground floor Jones casually mentioned they were going for a swift drink and invited Bare to join them. He would have preferred to just go with Sharon but accepted in the hope that Jones might disappear after the first round. Without even considering an alternative venue they made their way to the Swan and Bare's entrance was inevitably greeted with a loud cheer. Jones' puzzled expression caused Brady to whisper something in his ear and the senior detective slowly shook his head in reproachful understanding.

With the pub close to capacity the three stood with their drinks in hand at the bar as all the seating areas were already occupied. They were therefore limited to small talk which probably satisfied them individually for different reasons. It wasn't until the third round of drinks that Bare resigned himself to the fact that Gareth Jones had no plans to leave prematurely. It was at that point he also began to take note of the body language of his drinking companions. It was subtle and he suspected both were attempting to mask it but it was a dance he himself had performed so many times before that he could not fail to recognise it.

When Jones excused himself to visit the 'Gents' Bare used the opportunity to confirm his suspicions. He leaned forward and spoke quietly in her ear.

"So how long have you and Mr Jones been together?" he asked with that infuriating smirk she recognised so well.

"What? Oh don't be so stupid, we're just mates," came the reply she knew to be futile.

"Ah, don't worry, your secret is safe with me," replied Bare with a knowing wink.

"Well it makes a change for me to have a secret. Besides, it's very early days," she said and playfully punched Bare on the arm.

Although her reaction caused him to laugh her confirmation of his suspicions seemed to amplify his melancholy. He had no desire to rekindle his previous relationship with Brady but somehow felt sad that she was no longer exclusively his friend. He watched Jones walk back toward them and realised the senior detective was probably better for Brady than he had ever been so raised his glass to herald his return. Jones acknowledged the greeting without understanding its meaning and the small talk quickly resumed. At the end of the night the three departed the pub at the same time and each began to walk in the direction of their home. Bare suspected that the others would surreptitiously meet around the corner and he smiled at the memory of numerous similar encounters.

He briefly considered returning to the police station to collect his vehicle but was sober enough to realise how intoxicated he actually was and decided to walk home instead. The empty streets afforded any would-be assailant the perfect opportunity to attack him but he was unconcerned. In fact, part of him really wanted it to happen because he was certain that it was inevitable. He stopped momentarily and took a large lungful of the night air, wondering if he was being watched.

"Fuck me, Seb, you need to get a grip," he said aloud before putting his hands deep into his jacket pockets and continuing his journey home.

CHAPTER 51

His alcohol-aided slumber caused him to sleep though the alarm that had tried unsuccessfully to wake him for several minutes before admitting defeat and retuning to silence. When he did wake the unusual pattern of sunlight through the partly closed blinds in his bedroom suggested it was later than it ought to have been. He scrambled on his bedside cabinet until he found his mobile phone and checked the illuminated time display.

He mouthed a silent 'fuck' but made no effort to lift his aching head from the pillow, realising no amount of haste would get him to work on time. He hoped that his deputy would be covering for him at 'morning prayers' and he decided he would bluff the fact that it was always his intention to work a late shift.

He took a much longer shower than normal in an effort to somehow combat his hangover using the 'steady jet of warm water to the face' technique he had invented in his twenties. It didn't work and he reluctantly dried himself and dressed. Whilst the kettle was boiling he cursed as he was unable to find the box of paracetamol he vaguely recalled seeing weeks earlier. Bare rarely took any medication unless it came in a bottle with a label verifying its alcohol levels but his head was pounding. He found it puzzling given the relatively 'moderate' session in the pub the previous night. Then whilst still on the medicine hunt he saw the empty wine bottle beside the sofa and remembered his solo nightcap.

He aborted the search and settled instead for a black coffee, having also belatedly remembered there was no milk in his sparsely stocked fridge. His sobriety allowed him to reflect on the previous evening and specifically Sharon. He hoped that her embryonic romance would not affect their friendship and realised how reliant he had been on her over the last twelve months. Knowingly or not she had been his confidante, his sounding board and perhaps even his conscience. He in turn had probably done little for her which was another thing for him to feel guilty about. He hoped that she would one day forgive him for exploiting her support for his own gain.

He had a multitude of pending tasks that could have easily filled his morning but instead decided to walk to the local supermarket to replenish stocks. He hoped that the fresh air would be as effective as any over-the-counter medication and in truth he probably needed the exercise.

Upon emerging from the store with two fully laden bags of impulse buys he regretted his decision not to bring transport. There was a momentary consideration to wave down a patrolling police car but that would have probably constituted an abuse of authority so he started walking instead. The cheap plastic bags he had purchased weighed heavily as he made his way home and the handles began to cut into his hands. He stopped by a bench and searched through one of the bags until he found the headache tablets and took three with the assumption that the suggested two would be insufficient. He washed them down after opening a carton of milk and cursed his lack of planning. The only other liquid in his shopping came in the form of a six pack of lager which he did briefly consider.

When he reached the apartment block someone exiting the building kindly held open the communal door to aid his entry. Initially he was pleased to be the recipient of the kind gesture but then realised the person holding the door was one of his neighbours that he always strove to dodge. Eric wasn't a bad person but had the habit of wanting to engage Bare in long-winded inane discussions about the state of the world. These were normally prematurely ended by Bare explaining apologetically that he was late for work and rushing off with a promise to 'catch up later'. On this occasion, however, he was stuck and feared the worst as Eric had the appearance of a man with all the time in the world to put the world to rights.

Then with fantastic timing, just as the man enthusiastically greeted his neighbour, Bare's phone rang.

"Sorry, I'm going to have to get that, probably a work thing, catch you later," said Bare, now holding the entry door open to facilitate Eric's exit.

"No problem, we must catch up soon," promised the departing man resolutely.

Bare answered the call in the full expectation it would be someone from the station querying his whereabouts. Instead he was shocked to hear the voice that had he had heard only in his dreams for the last year.

"Hello, Sebastian. Long time no speak," said Avery.

CHAPTER 52

Bare tried to formulate a reply but the whirlwind spinning in his mind prevented any words coming out. When, after what seemed like a full-term pregnant pause, he finally spoke, he heard himself ask the most unnecessary of all questions.

"Who is this?"

In reply all he heard was laughter which confirmed the absurdity of the question that he nevertheless asked again.

"I said who is this?"

The laughter stopped and this time it was the caller who paused before answering.

"It's Paul Avery. Surely you haven't forgotten me already?"

The acceleration of Bare's heartbeat felt like it was going to cause a cardiac arrest but perversely he now felt composed enough to continue the conversation.

"Paul Avery was a worthless piece of shit and is dead," he said.

To his annoyance the insult seemed to provoke more laughter before he once again heard the familiar measured tone of Avery's voice.

"Well you never were the brightest of detectives, Sebastian, but I think even you are now doubting that fact. Tell me, how many times have you seen me in the shadows since we danced on that ledge?"

"What do you want? I knew you were responsible for the recent murders. They had your cowardly fingerprints all over them," snarled Bare, his rising anger evident.

"Of course they were my work, I even spelt them out for you as I anticipated you would struggle with the investigation. **A** for Amelia, **V** for Victor, **E** for Eve and **R** for Raymond the eunuch," laughed Avery. "Now, Detective Inspector Bare, as your name doesn't work very well we will just have to say the last person on my list is **You**."

"Well that's very neat, so what are you waiting for? I seem to recall last time you tried that it didn't work out too well for you," said Bare. As he spoke he found himself looking all around the apartment lobby in the expectation that Avery was in close proximity.

"Yes you are of course right, Sebastian. What did we used to say, the six Ps, was it?" asked Avery.

In an instance Bare was transported back to the briefing room where cops gathered before executing a search warrant. Whenever he or Avery had drafted an Operational Order they always shared the same mantra: 'Proper Planning Prevents Piss-Poor Performance'.

"You must have a good plan if you're confident enough to warn me in advance. Surely a knife in the back is more your style," goaded Bare in the hope of provoking an unguarded response.

"I'm very confident that by the end of the day the '**Y**' in my little mnemonic will be dead. You see, it will either stand for 'You', or if you prefer it will be 'Your son'. Just like that night on the cliff, Sebastian."

CHAPTER 53

Bare once again struggled to control his rising temper but realised he could not risk the conversation being curtailed before he could draw Avery out. He listened intently in case there was any background noise that gave a clue as to the man's whereabouts.

"What are you talking about? I don't have a son. You murdered my unborn child," said Bare.

"I honestly didn't know Julia was pregnant. She looked magnificent, naked on your bed. You were truly a lucky man, Sebastian. But you know it's not that child I am referring to, it's young Cameron. It's unfortunate his name doesn't start with a 'Y' but there again not many names do. I suppose they could have christened him Yogi but that might have been too much of a clue as to the identity of his real father, don't you think, Mr Bare?" laughed Avery.

"Where are you?" asked Bare without any expectation that Avery would answer truthfully.

"Or Yorick, then I could say, 'Alas I knew him well,' but I don't suppose Shannon and Liam were overly influenced by Shakespeare. Sorry, Sebastian, I'm digressing, actually I am quite close by. Can't you hear the seagulls?" replied Avery, enjoying every second of the conversation.

Bare remained silent, waiting to discover the purpose of the call. He could clearly now hear the sea birds referred to by Avery in the background and wondered whether the man was indeed close by. The rugged coastline where he had last seen Avery was less than two miles away and the memory of that night momentarily replayed in his mind. The short period of silence was broken by the sound of Avery's voice again; this time he sounded more businesslike.

"Sebastian, I have young Cameron in my custody and control. My proposition is very simple; it's you or him. Make your way to the Wellington statue immediately and I will call you with further instructions. You have fifteen minutes to get there. By all means make a call to Scotland to corroborate what I have told you but do not call local colleagues for assistance. If you do I will know and the boy will die. I have eyes and ears all around you, Sebastian. It's your choice."

Bare began to respond but realised the call had been terminated. He bent down and held his knees, breathing deep lungfuls of air whilst trying to process what was happening. Whilst remaining in that position he heard himself scream a series of expletives for no other reason than the need to expend some nervous energy and regain focus. When he again stood upright he saw a rather bemused-looking fellow resident who had entered the lobby from the street outside. Bare mumbled an apology and rushed outside himself whilst speed dialling the number programmed into his phone.

The call was quickly answered and he heard the polite Scottish accent.

"This is Ambleside School, how may I help?"

"This is Detective Inspector Bare, Operation Stockmarket. Is Cameron McKenzie at the school?" he shouted.

"No, Cameron was collected about an hour ago by your colleague Detective Sergeant Brady. Is everything okay, Inspector?" came the almost hesitant reply.

Bare didn't answer but merely terminated the call before immediately calling another number.

"Hello you, did you oversleep?" laughed Brady.

"Where are you, Sharon?" he asked in the breathless tones of a man who sounded like he was running.

"I have actually just been in your office looking for you. You need to brief your deputy if you're pulling a sickie," she laughed.

"Did you tell anyone about Stockmarket?" he asked.

"No, of course not," she replied emphatically.

"Not even Gareth?" he probed.

"No, nobody. I mean, I would never," she replied but was unable to finish the sentence as Bare spoke over her.

"Sharon, just promise me if anything happens that you will look out for my son," he said whilst negotiating moving traffic as he crossed a busy road.

"Are you still drunk? You know I promised that. What's happened, Seb? You're starting to worry me," she whispered, anxious not to be overheard.

"It's okay, nothing I can't sort, don't worry," he replied and immediately depressed the red 'end call' button.

He leant against the base of the large Duke of Wellington statue situated at one end of the busy High Street and took a series of deep breaths, regretting his lack of fitness. He checked his watch and exactly fifteen minutes after leaving his apartment the phone still clutched in his hand rang again.

CHAPTER 54

Sharon Brady tried to ring him back but the call diverted immediately to voicemail, indicating his phone was either off or he was on another call. She left a message requesting he call her back but stopped short of saying it was because she was worried about him. After initially returning to her own office she found herself unable to concentrate on work so sought out Gareth Jones. When she tracked him down she saw he was talking to the Senior Forensic Officer and overheard part of their discussion which appeared to revolve around the cost of some forensic submissions to the laboratory. Knowing this would not be a brief dialogue, she turned on her heels and made her way back to her office.

Her troubled expression must have been more apparent than she imagined as she was stopped in the corridor by a concerned looking Sarah Woodham.

"Are you okay, Sharon?" asked the Superintendent.

"Erm, yes, I'm okay, ma'am," came the unconvincing reply.

"Good, let's go for a coffee and a catch up then," commanded the senior officer.

Brady was aware that others at the station, specifically Bare, had misgivings about Woodham, but she had grown to like the woman. She seemed very intuitive and exuded a calm confidence in her command. They ordered take-out coffees and returned with them to the Superintendent's office, talking en route about holidays, a subject instigated by Woodham.

Once inside the office and with the door firmly shut the subject rapidly changed.

"Okay, so what is really troubling you, Sharon?" asked Woodham.

Brady hesitated, feeling conflicted between her loyalty to Bare and the concern his recent call had caused. She regretted agreeing to the meeting and wished she had been more patient waiting for Gareth Jones to become free. However, now feeling increasingly pressurised to fill the uncomfortable vacuum she heard herself speak.

"It's DI Bare, ma'am, I think he's pursuing something or someone and it's a bit off the books. I'm worried about him."

Woodham smiled in the knowledge there was no turning back for the junior officer now and she was about to learn what her maverick Detective Inspector was up to.

"Sharon, you are doing the right thing talking to me. We can't afford for any of our staff to be running any black ops. Tell me everything you know."

There was a short delay whilst Woodham retrieved her notebook from a desk drawer, clearly intent on recording the information she was about to hear. The few seconds thinking time this afforded Sharon allowed her to formulate the words that would be largely the truth but designed to help Bare rather than completely sever his legs.

"I think DI Bare remains convinced that Paul Avery is still alive and is responsible for the murders of Eve Kent and probably Amelia Hann. Furthermore, I think he believes that Avery will now come after either him or the young lad Cameron McKenzie again," she said deliberately slowly, to allow the Superintendent to contemporaneously record her words.

When she had finished writing, Woodham looked up as a cue to Brady to continue, sensing more troubling detail was to follow.

"And I think that Seb, I mean DI Bare, may have had some contact with the McKenzie family to share his concerns," she added, causing the Superintendent to reproachfully shake her head.

"So in effect he is in direct contact with an OCG and is giving them unsanctioned 'threat to life' warnings?" clarified Woodham.

"Yes, and there's more," said Brady.

"Oh, I guessed there probably would be," replied Woodham.

"I think that whatever DI Bare is doing is coming to a head right now. He rang me a little while ago and it's hard to explain, ma'am, but I know him so well. He sounded like he was on to something and was…" Brady stopped, unable to articulate the emotion she had heard in Bare's voice.

"And was what?" prompted Woodham.

"Scared, I mean really frightened," said Brady.

CHAPTER 55

"You sound out of breath, Sebastian. Too many liquid lunches?" queried Avery.

"Where are you?" demanded Bare, in no mood for small talk.

"I'm looking right at you. Funny to think we used to walk up and down this street with our top hats on, swinging our truncheons. Seems like a lifetime ago," reminisced Avery.

Bare scanned his surroundings once more, taking care to study the faces of pedestrians in the busy town centre as they walked past him. There was no recognition so instead he began looking at potential surveillance sites Avery might have chosen. The myriad of shops, restaurants and other commercial properties yielded no clues. There were also a few vehicles parked in the street, including a couple of white vans, and Bare realised that any of these would provide covert cover for Avery. There was of course another possibility, that Avery was nowhere at all close and this was just a game being played at his expense.

Almost as though his tormenter was reading his mind he then heard Avery speak again.

"You're wondering if I'm really here, aren't you Sebastian? I mean how could I have picked up young Cameron from Ambleside School and made it down here from bonny Scotland so quickly? Well, that's a mystery, isn't it, but if I were in Scotland how would I know there was an attractive blonde wearing a pink top walking past you now?" laughed Avery.

Bare stared at the woman walking past, causing her to smile in involuntarily politeness as she hurried past. The confirmation of Cameron's school name was not lost on him as he again surveyed everything around him.

"The boy is safe, you're bluffing, it's clearly me you want, not him," said Bare, slowly walking toward a parked white van that was currently his best bet.

"The boy is far from safe, as you well know by now, and I wouldn't come any closer if I were you," warned Avery.

Bare's patience was wearing thin so he ignored the warning and accelerated toward the van that was now starting to move off from its parking space. It appeared to have only the driver in the front but his appearance was indistinguishable as he was wearing a baseball cap and a blue surgical-type facemask. Bare reached the side of the van just in time and immediately opened the driver's door, causing him to drop his phone in the process. The driver, shocked by the unexpected interruption, slammed on his brakes as he felt himself being pulled out of the van. The seatbelt prevented his untimely exit and as he vehemently voiced his objection he felt his facemask being ripped off.

Bare stood in silence as he stared at the stranger before he belatedly identified himself as a police officer and apologised. Given the circumstances the driver, a man in his mid-fifties, surprisingly accepted the apology with relatively good grace. Bare retrieved his mobile phone from the road surface and saw it now had a cracked screen. He put it to his ear in the hope that it was still working and the laughter he heard told him it was.

"Oh, Sebastian, that was unexpectedly entertaining. You were lucky that man didn't punch you. What were you thinking ?" mocked Avery.

Bare was breathless from the encounter with the driver and suddenly aware that his actions had attracted the attention of several bystanders. He held up his police badge by way of unspoken explanation before managing to speak into the handset.

"What the fuck do you want?"

He was initially met with silence, causing him to check the display screen to confirm he had a continued connection. Then Avery spoke again.

"Let's stop playing games. Come and find me, let's talk face to face."

"Tell me where you are then," said Bare.

"I'm really surprised you haven't guessed by now. Don't you remember those night-time observations our Sergeant made us do? What was his golden truth?" asked Avery.

"People never look upwards," remembered Bare and in an instant he knew where Avery was.

CHAPTER 56

When Bare was a young Constable his Sergeant had been a worldly-wise, experienced police officer. His mantra was always that to be a successful police officer you needed to have 'local knowledge'. This meant knowing everything you could about your beat and its inhabitants. In a world without sat-nav this involved having knowledge of every shortcut, every alleyway and every accessible roof, particularly in the town centre. For nightshifts the Sergeant would routinely assign one or two young Constables to 'sky patrol'.

The design of the High Street meant that either end of a long parade of shops had accessible flat rooftops via an ornate spiralling metal fire escape. Once you had ascended the stairs and gained access to the first roof it was possible to walk along the entire High Street if you were brave enough to take the occasional small jump between buildings. By peering over the front-walled edge, officers on rooftops, would have an unrivalled view of the High Street below. It was a perfect place from which to conduct covert observations, as his Sergeant always said, "People never look upwards." Health and Safety legislation that came into force subsequent to those halcyon days had caused the patrol strategy to end. Whole generations of police officers had since patrolled the area without any knowledge of how their predecessors had worked as human CCTV systems.

Bare was surprised to see that the old fire escape still existed but noted that it differed in one significant detail to the one embedded in his memory. He vividly recalled the older version started at ground level, whereas the one he was now staring at seemed to be devoid of the first ten feet of stairs. Presumably these had been removed at some point to prevent any casual trespassing and he wondered how Avery had overcome this. It was possible that Avery had used an intact stairwell at the other end of the street, he surmised as he considered his options. He looked around the alleyway for inspiration and saw an industrial-sized wheelie bin that could easily be manoeuvred below the fire escape. Without a viable alternative he managed to wheel it in place and then clambered on top of it in a less than graceful fashion. His progress was interrupted by a ringing phone and he wondered if it was Avery calling again. The display was intact enough for him to see it was D/Supt Woodham's name in lights so he rejected the call. He did, however, send a text before replacing the phone in his pocket and finally got onto the bottom step.

The stairwell was higher and steeper than he remembered. It also showed no sign of any recent use, making him question whether he had arrived at the correct answer to Avery's riddle. Adrenalin rather than fitness fuelled his climb and Bare ascended to the first rooftop. He took a deep breath and surveyed his elevated surroundings. There was no sign of Avery as he slowly walked across the flat concrete toward the front of the building. He noted that there was a waist-high safety barrier now in place which took away some of the jeopardy as he looked down at the street below. Pedestrians were bustling around, moving from shop to shop, oblivious to his presence some seventy feet above them.

Bare walked slowly along the rooftop toward the middle section, wondering whether Avery would approach from the opposite direction. He visualised a modern-day version of two gunslingers on a deserted dusty street and wondered how foolish he had been to arrive with nothing in his holster. He consoled himself with the notion that whatever Avery had planned, it would probably not include allowing Bare a free shot at him in any case. It was difficult second guessing the intentions of a psychopath but Bare felt he had no alternative at this stage.

Bare's phone rang again and this time he answered it immediately.

"So glad you made it, Sebastian," said Avery.

Bare swivelled around but could still not see the whereabouts of his caller despite it being apparent he was in Avery's sight.

"Where are you then? You too afraid to come say hello?" he asked.

"I decided to try the other side of the street for a change. Look, I'm waving now," came the reply.

Bare was confused as the various buildings on the other side of the street were completely different in design and did not share any communal roof space. Then his attention was drawn to the multi-storey car park situated diagonally opposite him. He was unable to see the top floor due to the height differential between the buildings but on the floor more or less level with him he saw the waving man. The figure was partially obstructed by the design of the exterior wall and too far away to positively identify but Bare had no doubts as to whom he was looking at.

CHAPTER 57

As Woodham finished her radio transmission she saw Brady had arrived at her office, presumably armed with the information she had been tasked to acquire. The Superintendent raised expectant eyebrows, signalling she was ready to receive whatever Brady had found.

"So I tried to contact Cameron McKenzie's school but there was no response, I think they may have finished for the day. I also rang the local nick and there have been no reports of any incidents. They are happy to do a welfare check at the home address but I've asked them to hold off at the moment. Maybe I'm overreacting?"

"I trust your instincts, Sharon, and Mr Bare still hasn't turned up for work or answered his bloody phone, so you were right to come to me," reassured Woodham.

"So should I sort the welfare check? It might raise some questions from Mary McKenzie," said Brady.

"Get an FLO to do it, that way we can say it's just a routine follow-up," ordered Woodham.

Brady nodded and wished she had thought of the tactic of using a Family Liaison Officer. Despite her admission of potential overreaction she was glad that the Superintendent was clearly giving credence to her concerns. She suspected that if this turned out to be nothing, Bare would be less understanding. She waited a moment to see if there were to be any additional instructions but Woodham had already picked up the phone so she turned to leave the office. As she reached the doorway she couldn't help overhear that Woodham was arranging to get Bare's phone 'pinged' to identify his exact whereabouts. Once again she momentarily pictured his annoyance before she hurriedly made her way back to the sanctuary of her own office.

Having briefed a counterpart in Scotland, Brady felt confident that the enquiry at Mary McKenzies' house would be handled in a sensitive manner. She considered sending another text to Bare but guessed given his incommunicado status that it would be futile. Instead she stared at her own mobile screen, uncertain as to what to do next. Her preoccupation caused her to fail to notice the arrival of a visitor.

"Penny for them?" said Gareth Jones.

Brady smiled in response to the unexpected intervention. She felt increasingly comfortable in this man's presence and hoped that the feeling was mutual.

"I may have put the balloon up," she said, whilst pulling an exaggerated self-reproachful expression.

"Oh, do tell," smiled Jones whilst slowly closing the door behind him.

"I spoke to Seb Bare on the phone earlier; he seemed really worried and he hasn't turned up for work. I don't know what's going on exactly but I think Seb is convinced Avery is still alive and coming after him," she explained.

It took all of Jones' self-control not to roll his eyes in a sign of frustration that he sensed Brady would not appreciate. Instead he murmured something neutral before trying to echo the concern clearly felt by Brady.

She had intended to confide in him fully but checked herself at the last moment before revealing she had relayed the information to Woodham. This time it was impossible for Jones to suppress a micro-expression which told Brady he felt this had been unwise.

"Hence why you feel the balloon is well and truly up," he summarised and she nodded in regretful acknowledgement.

CHAPTER 58

Now that he had confirmed Avery's location, Bare managed to hurriedly send a further surreptitious text message, confident that his manoeuvre was covert enough not to be observed from across the street. When he returned the phone to his ear he was gratified to hear that Avery's monologue remained in full flow. He patiently waited for the inevitable ultimatum that was surely coming but was at least grateful for the time he was buying.

"So have you worked out what I want yet, Sebastian?" asked Avery.

"Why don't you just tell me, you wanker?" came the curt reply, causing Avery to laugh in the knowledge he was provoking an angry reaction.

"I'm just correcting a mistake you caused me to make, Sebastian. Remember on that cliff edge I gave you the choice as to who was going to die, you or (as it turns out) your son. You cheated me out of a death that day but here we are, same circumstances, same choice, you or Cameron."

"But Cameron isn't here," stated Bare flatly.

Avery almost admired the calmness of Bare's statement and was enjoying the fact that it was extending the dialogue. He was looking forward to replaying each exquisite detail in his mind when remembering the events that led to the demise of Sebastian Bare.

"But you know I have him in my control, Sebastian, you have by now verified that fact with your extended family in bonny Scotland, have you not?" taunted Avery.

"So tell me how you found out about him. Who gave you the information?" demanded Bare.

"Well I can't deny I had help from within the police station but the revelation about your son and his whereabouts was entirely down to you, Sebastian," laughed Avery, happy to emphasise how Bare had contributed to his own downfall. "Now it's decision time. Simple choice, either jump off that roof or I will send you a live video link to the execution of Cameron."

"So that's how you persuaded ACC Kent to walk into the path of a speeding lorry," said Bare, finally understanding the circumstances surrounding the senior officer's death. "But then you murdered his daughter anyway so not much of an incentive for me to jump, is there?"

Avery hesitated, annoyed that Bare had pieced together what had happened before but more perturbed about the man's continued calmness. In the fervent hope it was merely bravado being exhibited, he pressed ahead.

"Sebastian, I have no interest in hurting a child. Your death will be my last act before the curtain falls, I have a new life waiting for me. I give you my word that if you jump the boy will live."

"Your word means fuck all, you're a pathetic coward," was the less controlled instant response.

The outburst reassured Avery and he decided to raise the stakes even higher by imposing a time limit on Bare's decision.

"Sebastian, I think we've done talking. You have precisely one minute to decide whether you want to always know you were responsible for your son's death."

The cold, impassive tone told Bare that Avery was no longer in the mood to chat further and against all his primal urges to the contrary he peered over the perimeter wall and looked at the bustling world beneath him.

Avery, too, adjusted his position slightly to ensure he had a perfect view, and he licked his lips in salacious expectation.

CHAPTER 59

After growing impatient with the apparently hesitant Bare, Avery could not refrain any longer.

"Time's up, jump or Cameron dies now," he shouted down the phone.

But Bare did not jump and in fact moved away from the edge and its precarious view of the street below. He waited for Avery's command to fade before replying with a softness in his voice that made Avery strain to hear.

"Do you know the ultimate irony of all this?" he asked and then pressed ahead without waiting for Avery's answer. "Julia is the reason I've caught you."

"I've just ordered your son's throat be slowly cut, you stupid bastard," shouted Avery in frustration, seemingly ignoring what Bare was attempting to tell him.

Undeterred, Bare continued. Now it was his turn to torment.

"You see, she gave me that air freshener for my car the same day she told me she was pregnant. The traffic lights were a reminder to slow down but Julia added her own modification. She replaced the liquid inside with her perfume. I guess it was a reminder to stop fucking around. I knew straight away when I got into my car it had been tampered with and it was pretty obvious who wanted to listen to my conversations. So I gave you something I knew you wouldn't be able to resist."

There was a silence and Bare wished he could view the expression on Avery's face as he processed the information. After what seemed like an eternity he heard the man speak again. This time there was less anger and more of a disbelievingly disappointed tone.

"You mean you used your own son to bait a trap for me?"

As Avery uttered the words he slowly turned around in response to the shouted challenge behind him. Two armed police officers had emerged from a stairwell door and were slowly approaching him whilst simultaneously barking instructions. Avery turned his back to them and ignored the increased volume of their commands this action provoked.

"Well played, Sebastian," he said.

"Your turn to make a decision. A lifetime in prison or 'death by cop'," said Bare before terminating the call.

Avery closed his eyes in serious consideration of the choice he had to make. The second option Bare had referred to was a well-known form of suicide which he could easily instigate with a sudden turn and reach inside his jacket for an imaginary gun. It wasn't the lifetime of prison that frightened him but the utter humiliation of being caught. He knew he had only a couple of seconds to decide judging by the frantic shouts of the approaching officers. With a weary sigh he sank to his knees with his arms outstretched to signal his submission.

Bare had a limited view of proceedings from his position and took the absence of any gunfire as a sign that Avery had been captured. He took a series of deep breaths in a futile effort to quell his growing nausea, which the stress of the situation had caused. In an admission of defeat he bent over and vomited and the physical relief this caused allowed him to slowly regain some composure. In truth he had no idea how the scenario was going to play out and certainly didn't feel the euphoria he had anticipated at its conclusion. He sat down on the rooftop and used the small perimeter wall as a back rest, taking a moment to reflect.

The moment turned into ten minutes of contemplative

introspection as he stared at the cloud formations above him. If he had belief in an afterlife he would have tried to recognise Julia's face amongst the indecipherable patterns above him. But he had no faith so only saw an increasingly dark sky that forewarned him of an inevitable downpour in the near future.

As he slowly clambered to his feet he suddenly became aware of uniformed figures approaching him from different directions. He recognised a couple as being part of an Armed Response team and saw that although not pointed in his direction their guns were drawn and ready to deal with any sudden threat. Behind them he saw another familiar face, still in civilian attire but wearing some police emblazoned body armour.

"You okay, Seb?" she shouted.

"Yes, I'm fine. What the fuck are you doing here, Sharon?" he called back.

CHAPTER 60

The handcuffs behind his back were left in that position as Avery was placed into the rear of the unmarked car. He was going to protest that protocol demanded they be adjusted to the front stack position for prisoner transportation but instead remained silent. He guessed that any sign of dissent aimed toward former colleagues would not be looked on favourably given his offending record. The escorting officers had not uttered a word since apprehending him and he assumed their heroic deeds in capturing Britain's 'most wanted' were on hold until he was safely in a cell. The idiots had not even formerly arrested or cautioned him, a fact they would undoubtedly lie about later when legally challenged.

Avery stared out of the window as the vehicle sped away from the town centre, wondering whether he would ever witness the bustle of everyday life again. He was silently remonstrating himself for the mistakes that had led to his capture. Surely the biggest of these was recruiting an accomplice. The messages from her burner phone had clearly indicated that her mission had been successful and that Cameron had been quietly abducted from his school. Clearly she had walked into a trap and been apprehended herself. Then she had evidently co-operated with the police to allow the erroneous messages to be sent. She ought to have been smart enough to have somehow warned him and he vowed she would pay heavily for that betrayal.

As the journey progressed Avery's thought moved onto the inevitable trial he would have to face. One sure thing was that he would not go down without a fight. It would be the most grand spectacle the Old Bailey had ever seen and he would bring down as many former colleagues as he could. The thought of ACPO officers squirming at the prospect made him smile and reinforced the fact he had made the right decision to surrender his liberty rather than his life. Bare's career would certainly be over and he would enjoy seeing the pain he had caused replayed in his face as the pair stared at each other across a court room.

They would in time probably make a film about his escapades and some ambitious producer would seek an audience with him to gain insight into his mind. He would allow the meeting and drip feed clues about his unknown previous exploits which in turn would allow him to bargain for better conditions during his incarceration. Clearly he had a whole strategy to work out which would keep him occupied during the solitary confinement he was likely to be given.

Perhaps in time he could cultivate a network within the prison population. Initially that would be imperative for his physical protection but perhaps later it would evolve and enable him to commit acts in the outside world using some trusted agents. He would of course have to judge whether it was more beneficial to play the 'bad rather than mad' card but that would be determined by his surroundings. A secure hospital might afford more comforts than a prison but it wasn't an environment that held immediate appeal.

It was only when he noticed the journey was taking considerably longer than he was anticipating did he speak aloud for the first time.

"Can you tell me which police station we're going to?" he asked.

Other than the slightest of looks in the rear-view mirror by the driver there was absolutely no response to his question. Rather than antagonise the 'grunts' by repeating the question Avery just shook his head and resumed his silent narrative around future plans. The car turned onto the motorway and its speed increased accordingly.

CHAPTER 61

Bare accepted Brady's offer of a lift back to the station as apparently Ms Woodham was keen to debrief him. Both struggled to overcome the awkwardness of their encounter on the rooftop but Brady broke the uncomfortable silence first.

"Seb, I'm really sorry, it was just you sounded so strange on the phone and then when I couldn't get in contact with you I thought something bad was happening. I didn't expect Woodham to authorise a full-blown operation and ping your phone," she explained.

"It's fine, I think it all just got to me. I'm sorry I put you in that position. Did you tell her everything?"

There was no need for him to be specific as she knew immediately what he was referring to and she moved quickly to reassure him.

"I told her that you had a concern that Cameron McKenzie was at risk but obviously didn't disclose your relationship to him. I mean, I did try to call his school first just to be sure he was okay but couldn't get through to anyone. We've asked Police Scotland to do a generic welfare check at his home address," she said and hoped that her answer demonstrated the fact that she would never breach his trust.

Bare exhaled as he digested the information and attempted to process its ramifications. He was a skilled interviewer and knew he could continue the discussion without revealing anything unusual.

"Which school did you try and contact?" he asked.

"The one you told me to, Ambleside," she replied and wrinkled her nose, which he recognised as her typical nonverbal communication sign when she felt she was receiving an unwarranted challenge.

"Oh shit, sorry, I told you the wrong school. Ambleside was Cameron's original school, it's a tiny remote private one. He's now at a place called Oakwood which is much closer to his home. I'm sorry, Sharon. I haven't been thinking straight this past week," apologised Bare.

"Bloody hell, Seb, it's a good job I didn't get through. Can you imagine the confusion that would have caused?" she snapped, but didn't wait for an answer as she was keen to ask the question that was really bothering her. "So what were you doing on that bloody roof?"

Bare smiled as he realised what she was thinking and quickly responded to allay her fears.

"Don't worry, I wasn't ever going to jump, I just wanted to go somewhere familiar to think things through without interruption and for some reason 'sky patrol' popped into my head."

"And then I turned up with the bloody cavalry! I'm sorry," she replied.

"Yes, all very bizarre," concluded Bare.

"So did you get a chance to do your thinking before you were so rudely interrupted? Do you really think Avery is still out there somewhere?" she asked.

"I think I may have let my imagination get the better of me; irrational fears and all that. Deep down I know he is dead and can't hurt anyone anymore. I think recent events have just reopened old wounds," he said quietly and turned his head away.

"Hallelujah, I think it's really good that you are working things through, Seb. Maybe you need to speak to someone, there's no shame in it," she said and he felt her supportive touch on his leg.

"Yes, I think today has been pivotal. I feel things are going to be a lot better going forward," he agreed.

She smiled and waited for the irreverent addendum. Bare didn't disappoint as he vocalised a further thought.

"Do you think Woodham is going to charge this operation to my budget?"

CHAPTER 62

Avery had worked out something was amiss long before the car pulled off the road and onto a track that appeared to lead into a small copse. There had been no radio transmissions in the car, no chat and nothing at all familiar about the actions of the arresting officers. He had stolen a closer, furtive glance at the insignia displayed on the driver's epaulettes and concluded they looked less than authentic. His mind was working overtime but he figured that any display of his suspicions at this stage would not help him.

The car stopped in a small clearing and despite the gloom, exaggerated by surrounding trees, he saw another vehicle parked in apparent anticipation of their arrival. The white Ford Transit van flashed its headlights to welcome them as their car came to a stop directly in front. The car driver quickly stepped out and opened Avery's door, motioning for him to alight with a hand gesture.

Avery was determined to offer his captors no signs of any weakness, sensing they would feast on it. Instead he merely raised a contemptuous eyebrow and uttered a solitary word.

"Seatbelt."

His other escort, still sitting alongside him, realised that Avery could not get out of the car due to the restraint so leaned across and unclicked it. After waiting for the inertia mechanism to work fully on the belt Avery turned sideways and managed to step out without the assistance of his still-handcuffed hands. The driver had clearly grown impatient and hastened his exit by pulling one of Avery's shoulders forward with a sudden jerk. The action caused Avery to lose balance and he fell face forward with no hands to prevent the impact of his face on the solid ground.

He then felt a hand under each of his armpits and he was raised into a kneeling position before his hair was pulled backwards so that he could face the figures that had now emerged from the Transit van. The headlights of that vehicle were still on full beam so the people standing before him were almost in silhouette form but he could tell there were two burly males standing either side of a shorter female. When she spoke, her distinctive accent confirmed to Avery her identity but for the avoidance of doubt she introduced herself anyway.

"I am Mary McKenzie and I've been waiting to meet you for a very long time," she said whilst leaning forward and touching his face as if to confirm his physical presence.

Avery presumed this was to be the place of his execution and saw no value in responding to the introduction. Instead he stared defiantly at the woman and allowed the corners of his mouth to slowly curl up into a smile. This didn't appear to faze the woman at all as she stepped back from him and gave the two 'police officers' a specific set of instructions whilst they were changing into civilian clothes and placing their uniforms in a black bin bag. At her bequest one of them handed her his revolver and she checked it was loaded with a swift action that showed her familiarisation with firearms.

One of her companions then forced Avery to his feet and manhandled him towards a large oak tree, forcing him to then stand with his back against the large trunk. Mary McKenzie walked across and stood a few feet in front of him.

"You tortured and killed my two sons and daughter-in-law, you almost killed my grandson and you sent a deranged woman to kidnap him. You should have stayed dead," she said, raising the gun toward him.

"What do you want me to say? I think a lot of law-abiding citizens would just consider it to be pest control," said Avery.

If his words were meant to provoke a reaction they seemed to fail as Mary appeared unfazed by them. Instead she continued to stare at his face, perhaps seeking some true indication of his thoughts.

"They tell me you are a true psychopath and as such you are incapable of any feelings. Is that really true, Mr Avery?"

"Feelings and emotions make you weak. You're incapable of any true understanding," he replied but before he could speak further the crack of a fired gun interrupted him and he screamed at the searing pain that enveloped his right ankle.

"He seemed to feel that though," said Mary to one of her companions before handing the gun back to the man who had loaned it to her.

CHAPTER 63

After an exhaustive debrief with Superintendent Woodham, Bare returned to his office on the pretext of collecting some personal items. He had agreed to a period of annual leave as an alternative to her proposition of sick leave. He was confident that she was largely content with his explanation of events and was perhaps experiencing her own period of self-reflection around her response to the situation. Bare used a holdall from his locker to collect anything portable in the office that could remotely house some form of monitoring device before quickly returning to his car. He snatched down the air freshener from the interior mirror and added it to the contents of the bag before driving away. Only when over a mile from the station did he find a suitable place to park the car and walk toward the beach.

Satisfied with the seclusion of his surroundings he tapped the pre-recorded number and listened patiently to the ringtone before a familiar voice answered.

"This is Ambleside School, how may I help?"

"I'm really hoping you don't need to pretend to be a school anymore," said Bare.

"I wasn't sure if I was supposed to carry on answering that phone anymore. Are you okay, Seb?" replied Mary.

"Yeah, I'm fine. Is it done?" he answered, keen to get confirmation.

"It's done. The first one was in his leg for your wife, the others were for my family. I know it doesn't bring them back but I'm glad I got to pull the trigger."

Bare exhaled a sigh of relief. He wasn't surprised that she had taken personal responsibility for the task or that she had made him suffer. After digesting the information he sought clarity about the day's events, wanting to ensure there were no loose ends.

"I know it didn't exactly play out as we had intended. I was convinced Avery would have been up there with his accomplice. It was a good job the reserve team were down here. Tell me what happened with the woman."

"She turned up bold as brass flashing a warrant card and quoting Operation Stockmarket. Said she needed to take Cameron out of the school for his own safety. My boys were waiting and 'arrested' her. She took some persuading before sending him a text to say she had the boy. She cried like a wee baby for letting him down. The boys got her to admit her name was Sonia and she said she worked at your police station, Seb," explained Mary.

The revelation made sense to Bare and he realised that the new cleaner would have been perfectly placed to do Avery's bidding.

"I take it she has been taken care of too?" he asked with the full knowledge of the expected confirmation.

Sensing that the answer was less palatable to Bare she reminded him that the woman had clearly been heavily involved in Avery's murderous acts and had been fully intending to kidnap Cameron.

Bare acknowledged the justification and knew there could have been no other outcome.

"What about the bodies?" he asked.

"Sebastian, do you really want to know?" she replied.

"I am not sure I want to know, but I think I need to just so I can move on," he answered honestly.

"The family have a friend who is a trawler man, they will never be found. He was supposed to have died in the sea anyway," she replied matter-of-factly as though she was reporting back some everyday occurrence.

"Okay, speak soon," said Bare before terminating the call. He was glad the conversation had not taken place face to face as she would have witnessed his almost uncontrollably shaking hands. He took deep lungfuls of the fresh air as the wind blew inshore and tried not to think about the ramifications of his actions.

CHAPTER 64

Six Months Later

Bare was surprised how quickly things got back to normal. He was careful not to overtly display the complete serenity that he was now savouring as he wanted others to observe a gradual change brought about by a growing acceptance of circumstances. He had forgotten what it was like to enjoy the small moments that now seemed to increase by the day. His relationship with Robin was back on track and the distance between them ensured it progressed at a slow but steady pace, which suited them both.

He had only made one trip north of the border. As much as he wanted to spend time with Cameron he had found it difficult being in the company of Mary McKenzie. Although he had long known she had lived her life on the other side of the street, he had never witnessed or perhaps had chosen not to witness that aspect of her character. Her actions had demonstrated a cold ruthlessness that he found hard to reconcile with his manufactured view of a doting grandmother.

She had reluctantly allowed him to gift Cameron a games console which meant he could maintain a level of contact directly with the boy. Whilst getting his arse kicked playing an online football match, Bare was able to communicate via the console. He was careful to maintain a level of friendly text messages, knowing that she would invariably scrutinise the communications to ensure the pair did not become overly close. His only cause for paternal concern came when

Cameron told him he had successfully taught Tyrus an 'attack' command. This made him wonder whether the counsellor still seeing the boy on a monthly basis ought to be aware. Interestingly, during his visit Mary had instigated a conversation that suggested at some point in the future the boy should be told about his father. Although she had not specified a time period for this it was clear she was visualising a time many years ahead and Bare felt a sad acceptance of this view.

The romance between Sharon Brady and Gareth Jones had continued to blossom and whilst there had been no official announcement of their status it had become very much an open secret within the police family. Bare enjoyed seeing his friends happy in each other's company even if he utilised every opportunity to mercilessly tease Brady for dating an older man.

His position as a self-proclaimed 'desk jockey' continued to cause him some frustrations as he missed the cut and thrust of operational policing. His rank did, however, provide some advantages, most notably being able to nip in the bud some concern about the sudden absence of one of the station's cleaning staff. Her supervisor had raised concerns about Sonia's absence from work but Bare had been on hand to explain he had witnessed her verbal resignation. He had even concocted a whole 'backstory' to do with a move to a different part of the country but it had never been required. Bare had remembered one of his late mother's favourite observations on life when he had audaciously explained that his work had been too important to miss a family gathering.

"Sebastian, we are all just pebbles thrown into the water. Big ones cause a splash but when the ripples are gone you would never know they were there in the first place."

He had never fully appreciated her wisdom but now understood how transient life actually was, and he added not spending more time with her to his long list of regrets.

"Penny for them?" said Robin and he realised she had rejoined him in the airport departure lounge.

"I was thinking how lucky I am to be going to Paris for a dirty weekend with a gorgeous lady," Bare casually lied, deciding this was neither the time nor place to share his innermost thoughts about this mother.

"And what makes you think it's going to be a dirty weekend? I thought we were going to be culture vultures and just enjoy the museums and art galleries," she teased.

"You are absolutely right. Shall I ring ahead and change the booking at the hotel to two singles rather than a king-size double with ensuite private spa?" he asked.

"No, that's fine, I am happy to rough it sharing for a couple of nights," she laughed as she took his hand and skipped playfully towards the departure gate.

CHAPTER 65

The assembled police officers chatted amongst themselves before falling silent when the senior officer walked into the room. There was always an air of excited anticipation when a hastily assembled group of proactive cops were told to report for a 5am briefing. The hunters waited patiently to learn the identity of their prey and had already speculated that due to the numbers present, this was going to be an important target.

Unbeknown to the officers the information they were to be acting on had only come into police possession a few hours earlier. A well-known heroin addict had been arrested for theft and was keen to avoid the custodial sentence the judge had previously warned would be inevitable if he re-offended. He held, however, a 'get out of jail free card' that he was happy to trade for his liberty. It had come about because his sister was dating one of the infamous McKenzie family and had suspected he was not being entirely loyal in his affections. Specifically her cause for concern related to regular secret assignations where her boyfriend disappeared for hours on end without explanation.

She therefore employed her brother to covertly follow her man in the expectation that it would lead to the identification of her love rival. In fact the brother, surprisingly skilled at covert surveillance, had followed McKenzie to a very remote building set in the grounds of a private estate. Intrigued as to what was going on inside the building, the brother had established himself a vantage point and observed activity in and around the building. It didn't take him long to work out that he was looking at a very large cannabis factory. He even saw the standard accessory of a young Vietnamese 'gardener' taking a rare breath of fresh air by the front door.

Whilst not an expert in weed he was certain that such enterprises yielded thousands of criminal pounds. He was therefore able to placate his sister whilst retaining the intelligence he had gained for a rainy day. And yesterday it had poured. After he had been officially registered as a Covert Human Intelligence Source (CHIS) he was happy to offer the information in exchange for a generous acceptance as to how he had come into possession of some stolen jewellery.

The information had subsequently been disseminated to the officers tasked with dismantling various Organised Crime Groups in Scotland. It had been particularly well received as since getting their fingers well and truly burned in England, the McKenzie OCG had gone to extreme lengths to maintain their presence and activities closer to home. They notoriously ruled by fear and were very adept at covering their tracks. Therefore a gift horse potentially leading to the discovery of a large cannabis factory that no doubt funded other criminal activities could not be ignored.

The briefing to the officers was delivered in the form of a PowerPoint presentation and included various photographs of key members of the McKenzie OCG. It was explained that accompanying the officers would be an interpreter and representatives from partner agencies, specifically Customs staff and those with an expertise in Modern Slavery. Whilst there was nothing to suggest firearms would be needed the officer in charge alluded to the fact that specialist trained officers would be on standby in the vicinity, a fact always guaranteed to cause a murmur amongst the staff expected to enforce an entry.

The briefing quickly concluded as dynamic intelligence from a rural surveillance team reported the arrival of Tommy McKenzie at the site. This caused a palpable stir amongst those in charge as

Tommy, brother of the late Stuart, would be a prize capture. Within minutes the convoy was en route, armed with a search warrant and a voracious appetite. The lock on a perimeter gate was easily snapped and moments later the front door of the old brick barn burst open as the search team entered with shouted instructions aimed at anyone who might be inside.

Large polythene sheets were pushed aside to reveal a professionally assembled inner room that contained rows of nearly mature cannabis plants and a sophisticated hydroponics system in operation. The rapid entry technique employed had caught the inhabitants of the building completely unaware and they stood open mouthed as a seemingly endless number of officers followed each other in, each shouting indecipherable commands. Realising the futility of an attempted escape Tommy McKenzie merely stood and watched as officers approached him, casually sipping a coffee that his nephew Bobby had prepared for him upon his arrival a few minutes earlier. The nephew was less calm and picked up a nearby garden rake to use as an improvised weapon before yielding to related shouts to 'drop it' by the officers that surrounded him. Rather bizarrely the young Vietnamese gardener diligently attempted to continue in his duties with his head bowed as though whatever was going on was frankly nothing to do with him. Only when handcuffs were applied to his hands did he appear to realise that his work for the day had been curtailed.

CHAPTER 66

After the prisoners had been taken away, the painstaking business of a forensic examination of the scene began. More often than not this was the main hope of linking people to the scene but on this occasion there had been much proverbial back slapping because the officers had discovered not one but two of the OCG itself. Not only that, but in Tommy McKenzie they had probably landed a prized scalp they could scarcely have dreamt of. Given his contemptuous stare toward Bobby at the time of their arrest, it was fairly evident who he was going to blame for the discovery of such a well-hidden establishment.

A quick calculation based on the number of plants at the factory and their estimated yield produced a six-figure value on the establishment and the young Detective Sergeant in charge of the scene found it difficult to suppress a broad grin. He had endured enough false dawns and fruitless searches in the past to enjoy this exception to the rule. Gradually the numbers of officers at the site reduced until he was left supervising a handful tasked with dismantling the equipment and recovering the plants. The majority would be destroyed but a handful would be kept for evidential purposes. He was envious of the interviewing officers back at the station who would be tasked with interrogating the captured McKenzies and he wondered whether they would be able to break the traditional 'no comment' responses of hardened criminals.

The reappearance of the interpreter at the factory reminded him there had been a third prisoner. It was difficult not to feel sorry for the young lad, most likely to be an exploited and vulnerable illegal immigrant, often traded by OCGs and used as slaves to carry out menial and laborious work. He hoped that the lad was being treated well at the station and was therefore curious about the reappearance of the only man who had been able to converse with him.

"Sergeant, may I have a word please?" said the interpreter. His tone and demeanour was the personification of politeness.

"Yes, of course, what is it?"

"Something the young man said when he was arrested has been troubling me," explained Mr Pham.

The Sergeant recalled hearing the animated tone of the young man as he was being placed in the back of a police vehicle but had assumed it was merely a protestation of his innocence. He waited for the interpreter to clarify what had been said.

"He said that he was worried that the men in charge would feed him to the devil dog which they kept in chains in a dungeon," said Mr Pham.

The Sergeant smiled and placed a reassuring hand on the man's shoulder.

"It sounds like they made up some tale to keep him in line. I hope you told him there is no devil dog."

"Yes, I did, and at first I thought the same as you, Sergeant, but the lad was insistent and he said the dungeon was hidden by fire. It was only later I realised he didn't say fire but rather *the* fire," explained Pham, and then he pointed to the old feature fireplace on a side wall.

The Sergeant was intrigued enough to walk over to what he believed to be an ornate original feature of the building. It didn't appear to be anything other than a large brick opening and a quick look inside confirmed the chimney had long since been blocked off.

After he had inspected the old iron grate that was still in place he turned around and gave an apologetic shrug of his shoulders. Almost as an afterthought he lifted a dusty black rubber mat that had been placed in front of the old hearth and gulped as he saw that it had been strategically placed to cover what appeared to be an old trap door.

The Sergeant called over a colleague to help him slowly lift the hinged door and they were able to see a wooden ladder that descended into the blackness below.

"Go and get me a torch," the Sergeant instructed. Then as an afterthought asked his junior colleague, "What are you like with dogs, John?"

CHAPTER 67

Against his better judgement the Sergeant descended the ladder using the torch to ensure he didn't miss a step. His colleague above also shone a torch down in an effort to further help and it was his beam that illuminated the light switch. The Sergeant pressed the switch but there was no accompanying artificial light as had hoped. He then realised that before dismantling the hydroponic system officers had disabled the power supply as they were mindful of booby-trapped devices being used in the past.

"Fuck!" he exclaimed as he realised the torch would be his only friend.

As he stepped off the bottom rung and onto the stone floor he took a breath to compose himself. He immediately regretted the decision as an awful pungent smell entered his nostrils and he coughed in disgust.

"'You okay, Sarge?!" came the enquiry from above. "You want me to come down there too?"

"No, wait there," he responded and was sure he heard an audible sigh of relief.

With his back to the ladder but with one hand still touching it for comfort he slowly moved the torch around the otherwise pitch-black basement. It was difficult to gauge the room's size but it appeared to be rectangular in shape and he could tell he was at one end of it. As his torch moved around silently revealing the old brick walls he thought that the word 'dungeon' was an accurate descriptor. The silence in the room at least offered the consolation that the presence of a 'devil dog' appeared to be unlikely.

As the torchlight continued to pan around the sudden illumination of a shiny object at the base of a wall made the Sergeant suddenly stop. He took a couple of steps toward the object to assist his focus then gulped when he realised he was looking at a metal dog bowl. By moving the torch slightly to the left he then saw a heavy chain fixed to the wall at one end. Slowly his torchlight followed the chain from its fixed point along the basement floor until it disappeared into what appeared to be a large pile of old rags. Now confident no carnivorous beast was lurking in the shadows, he walked towards the rags and attempted to move some aside with his foot. It was only when he felt some resistance to his manoeuvre did he realise what lay beneath the rags and his urgent shout for assistance punctuated the silence.

"Can you get some more light down here now? I've found a body," he called.

In fact his colleague above then exceeded his request by managing to reconnect the building's disabled electric supply and a fluorescent light above him flickered into life. As his colleague clambered down into the now overly bright room the pair of them assessed the scene and realised that it was nothing more than a modern take on a medieval dungeon. The Sergeant didn't wish to disturb the crime scene any more than he needed to but as his prime duty was the preservation of life he made a token touch onto the body's neck to check for a pulse. To his shock the touch caused 'the body' to recoil away in the form of a very slight but definite flinch.

"Fuck, they're alive. Call an ambulance, and get some troops back here!" he shouted, causing his colleague to fervently speak into his lapel radio.

He then tenderly turned the now-still person below him over, whilst providing a continual reassuring commentary that he was the police and here to help. It was at this point he realised that he was dealing with what appeared to be a middle-aged man who was manacled around one ankle. The man's overgrown facial hair scarcely covered what appeared to be considerable trauma and swelling to his temple and area around one eye. He appeared to be breathing but was unresponsive to the Sergeant's questions, so the officer contented himself with just holding him in a semi-seated position until help arrived.

After what seemed like an eternity but in reality was less than thirty minutes, two paramedics descended into the basement and relieved him of his onerous responsibility.

"Is there anything I can do?" he asked to what appeared to be the senior of the pair.

"Some heavy-duty bolt croppers might be handy," said the paramedic, motioning toward the chain still linking his patient to the dungeon wall.

CHAPTER 68

Detective Superintendent Alastair Leighton made copious notes in his 'day book' whilst being briefed by the various officers involved in the search warrant and subsequent arrests. His appointment as the Senior Investigating Officer reflected the fact that the search warrant had yielded much more than could have been anticipated and now there was a golden opportunity to dismantle a notorious Organised Crime Group. The arrests of three men and the discovery of a high-yield cannabis factory were events enough to attract the interest of senior ranking officers, but the additional discovery of a mysterious hostage had piqued their interest further.

Leighton was, however, not distracted by the excited chatter of persons not connected with the case. He was a painstakingly methodical man and renowned for working at a pace others considered to be unnecessarily pedestrian. Even the arrival of a junior messenger desperate to relay dynamic information being received from the ambulance conveying the mysterious man failed to divert his attention. Instead he merely told the junior officer to wait until he had finished debriefing the Sergeant who had made the startling discovery. Only when Leighton was satisfied he had extracted and recorded all salient facts about events in the dungeon did he turn to the messenger who was putting weight on alternate feet in nervous anticipation.

"I take it you have an update, laddie?" he asked as he turned to a virgin page in his notebook in anticipation.

"Yes, sir. PC White has radioed in. The patient is conscious and the paramedics have allowed him to speak for a few minutes."

"And PC White is the name of the officer accompanying the ambulance crew, is he? Do you have his collar number?" asked Leighton.

The junior officer had thought he had been prepared for any supplementary questions the SIO might have but had not expected such a mundane one to start with. He looked down at his own book of hastily scribbled notes in the vain hope he had recorded the detail he was now being asked to provide. Leighton waited for a few seconds in frustrated silence before recording the name of PC White in his book whilst leaving a gap for the later insertion of the escorting officer's epaulette number. He then asked for a slow verbatim account of the update.

"The man has identified himself as being a Michael Warner, that's Whisky Alpha Romeo November Echo Romeo, sir," said the young man, attempting to deliver the message at the speed of Leighton's pen. "He says he was kidnapped because he owed a debt and then forced to work at the factory. He has no idea how long he has been there and says he got regular beatings by masked men. He won't say who he owes the debt to or what it was for and he can't or won't give up any names, sir."

Leighton recorded the account in his book and then patiently waited for the remaining information that was clearly waiting to be delivered.

"He has no idea where he is, sir, says he is from Manchester and that's where the kidnap happened as he was walking along a street. Says he was bundled into the back of a van and a hood was put over his head. The full extent of his injuries can't be assessed until they get him to the hospital but it does look like he has taken regular beatings. He also has fingers missing and it appears at some point he has been shot in the lower right leg. They should be arriving at the hospital about now, sir."

"Jesus," was Leighton's single-word response as he finished

writing the entry in his book.

Having ascertained that there was no other relevant detail to record he silently closed his book and called over the officers selected to interview those arrested at the cannabis factory. He instructed that the Vietnamese 'gardener' be interviewed first but reminded the officers to tread softly as it was likely that the detainee would end up being classified as a victim as well as a potential offender. He also asked that early contact was made with the Greater Manchester Police and that Mr Warner be kept under protective guard by PC White whilst being treated at the hospital.

Satisfied that everything was going in the right direction, he then returned to his own office and sat down at his desk. After taking a few moments to compose himself he opened his briefcase and took out a small mobile phone. He then stood up and decided to lock his office door for additional security before ringing the solitary number stored in the phone's memory. The recipient of the call quickly answered as though she had been anticipating the call but he didn't waste time with any pleasantries.

"Bloody hell, Tommy and Bobby have landed themselves in a right mess here. I'm not sure if there's anything I can do for them, they even had a tortured fucking hostage in a hidden cellar," he whispered into the handset.

"Tell me everything that's happened but let me be clear, Alastair, you will help them," said Mary McKenzie.

CHAPTER 69

The high-dosage painkillers were doing their job and the luxurious hospital bed made Avery want to stay in his private room forever. He had silently wished for death countless times in the preceding months but had never given those that held him the satisfaction of hearing his plea. When they had executed the sobbing Sonia in front of him he had made a point of yawning in feigned boredom just to demonstrate the futility of their actions. That had earned him a sustained beating and he winced at the memory of the repeated kicks to his ribs. His three missing fingers represented the members of the McKenzie clan he had eliminated and made him grateful his captors had not used this system to reflect the true number of all his victims.

As he lay in the bed his mind was filled with questions about his rescue. He had surmised that the police had stumbled upon him unexpectedly and the lack of handcuffs clearly indicated that they did not know who he was. He was unsure as to whether any of his tormenters had been arrested but presumed they would be in no hurry to divulge any information in any case. That said, the scraps of misinformation he had provided in the ambulance would not afford him much breathing space either.

As the door opened he immediately returned to pseudo sleep before establishing it was a nurse undertaking some checks rather than the uniformed Constable sitting outside his room. The nurse appeared satisfied that she had enough information to annotate on the chart hanging at the base of the bed and after a perfunctory click of her pen turned and left the room. The slow-closing door allowed him to overhear a snippet of conversation with the police officer outside which just seemed to be a general enquiry as to his welfare.

Avery put himself in the shoes of the officer in charge and knew there would be an impatience to harvest information from the rescued hostage. He was also acutely aware that any forensic evidence recovered at the scene could lead to his true identity being revealed which all pointed to the need for him to leave. It was only signage in the room together with his recollection of distance travelled when initially abducted that suggested he was in bonny Scotland. This of course made perfect sense to him given he had clearly been the guest of honour at some far-flung McKenzie residence.

After taking a few deep breaths he managed to shuffle into a seated position. He avoided putting any weight on his heavily bandaged left hand as he slowly swung his legs out of the bed. His right ankle area was also enveloped in a freshly applied bandage and reminded him that walking far might be a very serious issue. As he sat on the edge of the bed he felt interminably weak and he guessed he had lost at least two stone in body weight due to the meagre rations he had been allowed just to keep him alive. He was dressed only in a hospital gown and he shuddered having removed the bedsheets that had kept him warm. Using a bedside table as an impromptu balance aid he managed to shuffle over to the sink in the room. He gazed into the mirror above it and scarcely recognised the reflection that was staring back at him. His hair had grown into a straggled mess and his facial hair was very much in the style of a rough sleeper he so commonly encountered on the streets of London. He saw that the area above his left eye was still heavily swollen and discoloured and his nose now resembled that of a seasoned street fighter.

He tenderly touched his cheek and recalled that one of the blows that landed early in his captivity had caused an incisor tooth to fly spectacularly from his mouth. The accompanying laughter this had caused to one of those patiently awaiting his turn for a punch still rang in his ears. Avery didn't need to lift the gown to know that its flimsy material covered a whole host of scars and bruises that had been collected over recent weeks, each one testimony to a beating accompanied by scornful derision. Their lack of imagination about the nature of his torture indicated an amateurish approach that he had part despised but was also grateful for. It was only on those occasions when Mary herself visited did he feel particularly apprehensive as to what would follow.

He knew the only thing that had kept him alive was the obstinacy of his silent defiance, which had infuriated those that wanted him to beg for mercy. He also knew that such was the deep hatred that she held for him, it was likely someone had already been dispatched to finish the job before he was totally out of reach.

CHAPTER 70

As he stood transfixed by his mirrored image he heard the door open once more. This time it was the young uniformed Constable checking on his welfare.

"You're awake at last," said PC White as he closed the door behind him.

Avery turned slowly to face his visitor and quietly assessed the bright-eyed youthful man. He guessed the lad was probably still in his probationary period given his age, immaculate uniform and highly polished shoes. As he smiled to welcome his visitor Avery performed a series of mental calculations as to his best chance of killing the police officer and making good his escape. Had he been in peak condition he would have backed himself nine times out of ten but now he was looking at the optimistic reality of maybe a 5% chance of success.

Not liking his odds, he chose to shuffle back to his bed and try to buy enough time to think of an alternate strategy. PC White moved a visitor's chair to the bedside and presumptively got a notebook and pen out of his pocket.

"I wonder if you are up to providing a few more details now? As you can imagine we're keen to find out what's happened to you," said the officer earnestly.

Avery stared at the pen poised in the policeman's hand and realised it was a good quality metal biro. In the absence of other readily at hand alternatives it would make a good improvised weapon.

Maybe a stab to the eye or carotid artery? No, it would have to be the latter and he would somehow have to use his bandaged hand to smother any scream or call for help. So the attack would need to be quick and from behind.

"Mr Warner?" prompted the officer, eager to bring his witness back from the daydream state he had seemingly entered.

"Call me Michael. Mr Warner is what my pupils at school call me," said Avery in the softest voice he could muster.

"Oh, you're a schoolteacher?" said the genuinely shocked officer.

"Yes, and with a son about your age, although sadly he didn't make the same life choices as you did, young man," said Avery as he began to paint a verbal picture of an innocent, non-threatening man drawn into a foreign criminal underworld. "What's your first name, son?"

"Andrew," replied the officer instantly.

"No way, that's my son's name too!" exclaimed Avery, thankful the officer hadn't been christened with something more obscure.

"Can you tell me what happened, Michael?" asked PC Andrew White.

Avery spent the next thirty minutes recounting an elaborate story designed to endear him to the young officer and present himself as a gentle paternal figure. He explained that he lived alone in Manchester and had a difficult relationship with his estranged son he knew to be a drug addict. He was able to describe in detail how his son had become involved with a young woman who shared his addiction for those evil drugs that had ruined so many lives. Then one fateful evening about six months ago his son had called him begging for help as something 'terrible' had happened. He had of course responded to his son's plea for help and rushed to the flat where the son and girlfriend had been squatting. Upon arrival he had found the girlfriend had taken an apparently accidental fatal overdose that his son had helped administer.

PC White busily recorded the fictitious events into his notebook, hanging onto his witness's every word. When Avery tearfully revealed the surname of the deceased girl to be McKenzie and that she was somehow connected to a large crime family, the officer began to join the dots.

"We left that poor girl in the squalor and my son went on the run, knowing her family would blame him for her death. When they came looking for him I tried to reason with them but they wouldn't listen. They took me instead but I have never told them where my son is," concluded Avery.

"Why did you tell me in the ambulance that it was all because you owed a drugs debt?" asked PC White.

"Because even then I thought it might be possible to keep my son out of it. I'm so sorry, I wasn't thinking straight. If you have kids you'll understand."

The officer placed a supportive hand on his shoulder to demonstrate his empathy and for a split second Avery contemplated making his move, but then the door opened once more.

CHAPTER 71

The young Constable stood up to acknowledge the presence of a senior officer and Detective Superintendent Leighton was gratified he did not have to introduce himself to his junior colleague. PC White then attempted to introduce his boss to Michael Warner but the Superintendent appeared dismissive and almost aloof, even to the point of averting his eyes from the hospital patient.

"Let's go for a coffee and you can bring me up to speed," said Leighton, gesturing toward the door and then actually turning back toward it as though he was in a hurry.

PC White hurriedly followed, picking up his notebook but in his haste leaving his pen on the small bedside table where he had been diligently working. As he scurried to leave the room Avery jokingly ordered a cappuccino and the officer acknowledged the request which made the patient smile.

"Would you mind turning the main light off on your way out? I think I'll try and have a nap while you have gone," requested Avery and the sudden gloom in the room as White left indicated that he had complied.

Avery lay quietly for a few moments to process what had just happened. As far as he knew there was no police officer in the vicinity of his room and the Detective Superintendent had behaved oddly. Had he been the Senior Investigating Officer he would of course taken the time to meet a critical witness and use the opportunity to make a judgement about their credibility. But this man had appeared anxious and his reticence to even look at his witness had not gone unnoticed by Avery. The brief meeting had made Avery nervous and uncertain, reinforcing the growing desire to reclaim some control of his circumstances.

Meanwhile, as Leighton walked purposefully down the long corridor PC White kept pace alongside him like an eager-to-please puppy. The young officer was eager to impart his newly discovered information but first needed reassurance that it was okay to leave the key witness unattended.

"I think he'll be fine for a couple of minutes. Surely you've taken a comfort break yourself in the last few hours," reassured the Superintendent as he gave the faintest acknowledgement to a staff member dressed in full operating scrubs walking in the opposite direction.

PC White felt foolish for raising the matter and hoped the detailed explanation from Warner that heavily implicated the McKenzie crime group would provide some redemption. As they stopped at the coffee vending machine at the far end of the corridor Leighton took an age to read the simple operating instructions displayed on the machine. Finally he inserted a succession of coins from his pocket and turned to the young officer patiently waiting at his side.

"Well?" said Leighton.

"Oh, just a flat white for me, sir, no sugar," replied White before his face reddened with embarrassment upon the realisation that the enquiry had not been about his coffee choice.

As the senior officer waited for his own beverage to be dispensed, PC White filled the silence by relaying the account provided by the innocent schoolteacher who had merely been trying to protect his son. Leighton risked a premature sip of the hot drink and instantly regretted it as the scalding coffee burned his top lip. He cursed his own foolishness before allowing PC White to continue the story which made little sense to him. He knew the McKenzie clan well enough to know they would not go to the time and trouble of imprisoning someone for that length of time in the hope of extracting some information from them. He remembered the tone of Mary McKenzie's voice when he had told her where Warner had been taken. It was apparent to him she had not recognised the name given by the captive so there was clearly a lot more happening than either side were sharing at this moment.

Leighton hoped that his actions would fulfil his obligations to Mary McKenzie and that he could serve his remaining time in the police service without providing any more favours. Then he remembered the favourite saying of his late father, a lifelong supporter of the local perennially under-performing football team. 'It's the bloody hope that kills you, son.'

CHAPTER 72

The 'surgeon' quietly opened the door after a final check that nobody was witnessing his act. He was dressed in blue scrubs and wearing a face mask and protective hat as though he had just stepped out of the operating theatre. He was even wearing a pair of 'crocs' and carrying the obligatory clipboard to complete his disguise. The room was dark but he could see the outline of a sleeping patient under the bed clothes as he walked slowly toward the artificially high hospital bed. By now he had removed the primed syringe from his pocket and he realised his assigned task was going to be so much easier than he had anticipated. He knew that he only had a small window of opportunity before the abstracted police officer was due to return so could not afford to waste any time.

As he reached the bed he realised that it did not contain his sleeping target but just an arrangement of pillows designed to give that impression. But it was too late to react as a bandaged hand immediately covered his mouth and he felt a searing pain on the right-hand side of his neck. The would-be assassin did not have time to register what was happening as the attack killed him instantly but nevertheless carried on in a frenzied fashion for several seconds longer.

The exertion of his efforts caused Avery to momentarily lay alongside his victim before he too realised time was not on his side. Ignoring the newly returned pain of his own injuries he stripped the man of his clothing and placed his naked bloodied body in the bed that had been his own minutes earlier. He covered the man as best he could before adopting the persona of a visiting surgeon himself. He felt the presence of a wallet and some car keys in the trousers he was now wearing. These items provided him additional hope that his unlikely escape was possible as he slowly opened the door.

Save for the presence of an elderly couple walking slowly hand in hand the corridor was mercifully empty as he emerged into the harsh artificial light of the thoroughfare. They bade him a polite hello as he walked past, apparently unfazed by the sight of his freshly bloodstained hospital attire. He saw an unattended wheelchair in the corridor and gratefully took it to steady his walk as he made progress toward the signposted exit. Within a couple of minutes he was outside and breathing fresh air for the first time in months and he felt exhilarated. The fading light of the day made the blood staining on his outfit less conspicuous and he decided to take a risk and abandon the wheelchair as he approached the visitors' car park. For the first time he reached into his pocket and retrieved the keys from within. On the keyring was a chunky black remote emblazoned with a BMW logo and he depressed the button in the optimistic hope of hearing a waiting car dutifully responding.

At first he heard nothing but after walking between the rows of parked vehicles and repeating the process many times he suddenly saw the acknowledgement of flashing indicator lights. Without hesitation he opened the driver's door and within seconds he was driving toward the exit. A departing van allowed him to undertake a tailgate manoeuvre and dodge the descending barrier and then he was on a busy main road without a clue as to where he was. When it was safe to do so and after driving at least five miles he found a quiet spot to park. A quick check of the glove box revealed there was a switched-off mobile phone and a few other sundry items including a knife and a roll of black Gaffer tape. Quite the assassin's toolkit, he thought. He used some of the tape to alter the appearance of letters on the car's numberplates, a crude job that would not withstand close inspection but he hoped might confuse any ANPR cameras he passed. He hoped that his victim had been shrewd enough not to be associated with the vehicle in any case but you could never tell with amateurs. Avery then examined the contents of the wallet bequeathed to him and was happy that it contained some cash as well as a few plastic cards. It also contained a driving licence and he studied the photograph displayed on it. The image confirmed his suspicions that the man he had murdered that evening was the 'police officer' that had arrested him months earlier. He wondered if the man had a family waiting for him at the address on the licence and briefly contemplated paying them a visit.

But as quickly as the notion had popped into his mind it disappeared when he realised that he had more pressing priorities to safeguard his new-found freedom. Plus, there were a number of people who were higher on his list than some inconsequential members of a failed hitman's family. He restarted the car engine and noted it had nearly a full tank of petrol that would allow him to get several hundred miles away. He wondered whether this would be the most sensible option but instead he found himself reviewing the sat-nav's previous destination history. It showed a number of local places had been visited over the last few days and he realised that these addresses might be of interest to him.

CHAPTER 73

As the police officers walked back along the corridor, Leighton hoped that the diversion created had provided 'the surgeon' enough time to carry out his procedure and disappear. He was confident that he had enough experience to withstand the inevitable disciplinary enquiry that would inevitably follow with the worst outcome likely to be a reprimand for lack of diligence in protecting a witness. By the time that result landed he would be retired and living somewhere hot and peaceful. As they got closer to the private room he felt his heart beat faster in nervous anticipation as he wondered how clean the surgeon had been in his work.

PC White was carrying two cups of coffee that included the requested cappuccino, so it was down to the senior officer to open the door. The room was quiet and appeared to contain just a sleeping patient. Leighton wondered if the plan had been aborted and he found himself hoping that was the case. He had done his bit and if others had failed to capitalise on the opportunity then that was their problem. Any further attempts would have to make do without his assistance.

Then he saw the pool of blood on the floor by the bed and he realised he would have to adjust to a new reality. He stopped and waited for the inevitable as PC White gently placed the paper cups on the bedside cabinet. He saw the Constable look down at the sleeping patient and braced himself.

"Shit. Can you put the light on, sir? Something isn't right," called out the officer in what Leighton considered to be the understatement of the year..

"What's the matter, son?" asked the Superintendent as he dutifully illuminated the room fully.

If Leighton had been worried about feigning shock then he need not have been concerned as he and PC White stared at the dead stranger in the bed.

"Who the fuck is that?" he heard his junior colleague exclaim and he had no answer.

PC White looked at Leighton for guidance but all he saw was a man like him trying to comprehend what had occurred in the short time they had been absent. Although Leighton recognised the man as being someone whom he had met two hours earlier he was shocked by the grotesque sight now before him. For a few seconds there was a stunned silence before the experienced detective regained a level of composure.

"Right, this needs to be locked down as a crime scene. I want you on the door and running an incident log. Record the timings as best you can and note down anybody who comes to the room. Nobody to come inside until we get forensics here. I need to update Control and we need to find Warner or whatever his bloody name is. He can't have got far given the state he was in," ordered Leighton.

He looked at his uniformed colleague for confirmation or at least understanding of his orders but White appeared rooted to the spot, the shock of the discovery still registering in his mind.

"PC White, did you hear what I bloody said? Get a grip, man," barked Leighton.

"Errm, yes sir, sorry sir," said the Constable as he backed away from the bed, unwilling or unable to look away from the murder victim.

As the pair reached the door Leighton placed a conciliatory hand on his colleague's shoulder and spoke in softer tones.

"Okay, use your notebook as a temporary scene log and I will go raise the alarm," he said whilst struggling to get a signal on his mobile phone. "I need to get nearer the exit to get a signal, okay son?"

"Yes, sir. May I borrow a pen?" asked PC White.

"Have you not got a bloody pen?" replied an irritated Superintendent.

Instead of answering the Constable apologetically pointed to the dead body and Leighton realised the item protruding from the man's eye socket was a fully embedded metal biro.

CHAPTER 74

The weekend had flown by and Bare wished they could have stayed away longer, much longer. He had acquiesced to her wish that mobile phones should remain switched off for the duration of the break. At first it had felt like an unreasonable request but within a couple of hours he would have happily thrown the bloody device into the Seine as he loved the feeling of unrestrained liberty that being incommunicado provided. He also loved the way Robin shouted 'La Liberté' as she happily turned off her own phone and in fact loved most things she had done and said over the weekend.

As the pair emerged from the 'Arrivals' gate at Heathrow the plan was for them to spend one further night at her place in London before returning to their separate work lives the following day. It was only when he saw Robin turn on her phone that he reluctantly followed suit. The amount of missed calls and messages made him stop in his tracks as Robin walked on in an attempt to find a taxi. Bare listened to the succession of voicemails that became increasingly frantic and angry due to his failure to respond. After listening to the last of the messages he hurriedly caught up with Robin just as she successfully hailed a black cab.

"Look, I'm really sorry but I have to go, it's an urgent work thing, they've been trying to get hold of me," he explained whilst handing over her small suitcase but retaining his own.

"Oh, Seb, can't you say you didn't get the message until tomorrow morning?" she implored.

But she could tell from his expression and body language that she had already been relegated to second choice. Anxious not to end such a beautiful time on a sour note, she made no other plea but merely gave him the tightest of hugs before departing in the taxi that had been impatiently waiting. He waved her goodbye and instantly felt the guilt of perpetuating another deception, having resolved over the preceding couple of days to be more honest.

As soon as the taxi disappeared into the sea of vehicle lights flowing toward central London he returned to the terminal building but this time he sought out the Departures entrance. He sought out a quiet corner in the bustling Terminal and after a deep breath rang the number that had so urgently been trying to establish contact. Minutes earlier he had been blissfully happy but now he was experiencing a combination of disbelief, anger and trepidation. As he listened to the ring tone he realised it was important to stay calm but as soon as she answered he found himself breaking another promise to self.

"What the fuck have you done?" he demanded. Only his surroundings kept him from shouting the angry question.

"I am so, so sorry, Sebastian. I've made a terrible mistake," whispered Mary McKenzie.

Her tone and the sudden realisation she might be in the company of Cameron instantly dissipated his anger. He realised that his first question ought to have been whether the pair were somewhere safe. He then realised this was a superfluous question as whatever else she was, he was certain she was a devoted grandmother. After providing reassurances he was in no place to give, Bare requested she tell him everything. He then slumped into an uncomfortable airport lounge chair as she did just that. At this point she had recognised that there was no point in withholding any secrets so told him everything in accelerated detail. She tried to reassure him that it was not a premeditated plan to hold Avery a prisoner but that her rage at his defiance and her thirst for revenge had led to a series of irrational decisions.

Bare shook his head in disbelief as the sequence of events was explained to him. The police discovery of a location only known to trusted family, the arrest of her brother-in-law and nephew, the assistance of a corrupt senior officer and finally the disastrous 'hit' attempt at the hospital.

"And nobody knows who they are actually looking for? Not even your tame SIO?" said Bare, struggling to contain the incredulity in his voice.

"Nobody, just a few family members and now one of them is in the morgue. The cop up here obviously suspects I'm not telling him everything. He says that forensics are being done to identify him, they will have his DNA from the murder at the hospital."

Bare had a hundred more questions as he tried to process the information. He knew that Avery's criminality had largely been exposed after his believed death so the man's DNA wasn't on the national database. Fingerprints could be an issue but he was unsure as to whether Police Scotland would have access to prints of English officers that were routinely held for elimination purposes. He stopped thinking about all the hypothetical scenarios that could lay ahead when he realised it could rapidly become a tortuous process.

"Are you sure it's safe for you to be at home?" he eventually asked.

"Yes, I think so. So few people actually know where we live and I've imported some additional security until I can work out what to do next," she replied, the confidence in her voice providing him with some reassurance.

"Okay, sit tight, I'm at the airport and will get the next flight up," he replied.

CHAPTER 75

It was nearly 4am when Leighton arrived home. A new SIO had been appointed following events at the hospital but this was largely because he had become a witness himself rather than any accusations of corruption or incompetence. Of course he could have aided his successor by identifying the murder victim but naturally he chose not to. He had a concern that someone might have witnessed his earlier encounter with the man when they had concocted a plan that would leave Warner alone and vulnerable. But this encounter had taken place in his own private driveway, largely obscured from any nosey neighbours and had only lasted a few minutes. His wife was still away visiting her terminally ill mother so there was no casual observation from her either. In fact, given everything that had happened he allowed himself the indulgent thought that he had emerged from the whole sordid mess relatively unscathed.

He wearily opened the front door and was grateful that he was not expected back at work now for a couple of days. He was already looking forward to a lazy day tomorrow with hopefully no interruptions from either of his employers. He placed his briefcase down on the plush carpet and its soft landing was a reminder to slip his shoes off for fear of dirtying the new soft furnishing addition. As he bent down to untie his laces he was aware of a flurry of movement from behind and then almost instant pain to the back of his head. The carpet softened his fall but the bloodstain would prove problematic to clean.

When he regained consciousness it took him a few seconds to

realise he was sitting on his dining room floor with his back propped up against the wall. He instinctively wanted to rub his throbbing head but his hands appeared to be tied or taped together behind his back. He could see his ankles were secured together too by black tape that had repeatedly been wrapped around them. He presumed that it was another section of the tape that had been stuck across his mouth which prevented the verbal protest he so wanted to shout.

From his seated position he had a limited view into the kitchen but he could see that it was occupied by someone who appeared to be standing in front of his open fridge apparently perusing the contents. He tried to raise himself from his seated position but the restraints made it impossible. His movements, though, did attract the attention of his uninvited visitor who walked into the room from the kitchen casually eating one of the precooked chicken drumsticks that had been in the fridge.

Avery helped him back into a more stable seated position before inspecting the site of the man's head wound with his non-food-holding hand.

"You probably won't believe this but I really didn't intend to hit you that hard. I'm really sorry, is it stinging much?" he asked.

All Leighton could do was rapidly blink in furious indignation which Avery appeared to accept as confirmation his prisoner had now at least regained his faculties. He pulled a dining chair from beneath the table and sat backwards astride it so he was facing Leighton. For a few seconds he didn't speak and was seemingly more intent on finishing his snack, much to the bewilderment of the restrained man. After eating the last piece of meat from the bone, Avery then used it as an impromptu baton as though he was about to conduct an orchestra.

"I am going to ask you a number of questions that require a yes or no answer. So nod or shake your head accordingly. Do you understand?" asked Avery.

Leighton made no movement but his eyes burned with fury at his predicament which caused Avery to stand up and return to the kitchen. When he came back Leighton saw the chicken leg had been replaced by a large combat knife. This time Avery crouched down directly in front of his prisoner before repeating the same question. Leighton responded instantly by nodding his head.

"I'll be honest, I had no idea whose house I was breaking into but then I saw the lovely family photos on the wall and I remembered you from our brief time at the hospital. No sign of the lovely wife, though, has she left you?"

Leighton shook his head.

"Oh, are we to expect her back soon then?"

Leighton again shook his head.

"Okay, that's good, because I don't think it would be a positive experience for either of you if she were to return home. Do you understand?"

Leighton nodded his head but in truth did not feel that anything about the experience was likely to be remotely positive for him in any case.

CHAPTER 76

To assist his understanding of the situation, Avery patiently explained to Leighton how he had arrived at the address by looking at the sat-nav history of the car he had borrowed from its recently deceased owner. He also explained that whilst waiting for Leighton to arrive home he had taken the opportunity to borrow clothing from a well-stocked wardrobe, freshen up in a nice bathroom and been mightily impressed by the collection of fine wine on display in the dining room cabinet. He then asked if Leighton would be more comfortable if the mouth tape was removed and when he received another nod it was ripped off with an elaborate flourish.

"Now we can talk properly, much more civilised," said Avery.

"What the fuck are you doing in my house?" snarled Leighton.

The smile disappeared from Avery's face and he appeared genuinely disappointed with the angry demeanour adopted by Leighton. He replaced the mouth tape and moved the combat knife close to the other man's face.

"Don't mistake my kindness for weakness, you piece of shit. Speak to me like that again and I will cut you just for fun. Want to try again?"

Leighton nodded and the resigned look he gave allowed Avery to once again remove the mouth restraint.

"Do you know who I am?" asked Avery.

"You said your name was Michael Warner," replied Leighton, trying desperately not to say anything incorrect.

"That is, of course, a pseudonym. Who am I really?" persisted Avery.

"You are clearly someone who upset the McKenzies, but beyond that I have no idea," replied Leighton.

"Jesus, do you not have television or newspapers in Scotland? Who 'upset' the McKenzies by executing members of their family?" said Avery.

Leighton studied the face that was now inches from his own and tried to look beyond the mass of hair and injuries. The dawning realisation that he could only be in the company of one man caused an expression of genuine shock.

"It can't be, you're dead," he finally announced.

"And yet here I am and here we are, two Detective Superintendents with an interest in the same case. Do you want me to share a theory with you?" asked Avery.

Leighton nodded, unable to find any words. He of course was familiar with the story of what had happened to Mary McKenzie's family on the south coast maybe two years ago but it was completely incongruous to imagine that the dead psychotic cop was now in his dining room wearing his bloody suit.

"Well you're obviously in employ of the McKenzie family for financial gain or because they have something on you, or maybe a combination of both. But why would their hired hitman need to meet with you before coming to the hospital to finish off yours truly? I really struggled with that. Surely it could have been arranged over the phone as all you did was divert the uniform away from my bedside. Then I realised, that wasn't the original plan, was it? He came here to deliver this. You were supposed to do it, am I right?" said Avery whilst producing the syringe from his jacket pocket.

"I told him I'm not a murderer," said Leighton, his eyes firmly fixed on the item that he flatly refused to take hours earlier.

Avery fist pumped the air with obvious delight.

"I fucking knew it. Once a detective, always a detective," laughed Avery. "So tell me, did you even consider it?"

"No, it was bad enough having to open the door for someone else to do it. You won't believe it but deep down I'm a good cop," said Leighton.

"Which is why we are going to work together, Alastair, because we both want to be free from the McKenzie family, am I right?" said Avery.

Leighton had no idea whether the madman was right or wrong, at that moment he was unsure what day of the week it was, but he could see a glimmer of hope if he played along.

"You're right," he sobbed.

CHAPTER 77

The plane touched down at Glasgow a mere eighty-three minutes after leaving Heathrow but for Bare it seemed the flight had lasted a lifetime. The enormity of everything that had happened was beginning to sink in and he struggled to imagine an outcome that didn't involve his death or imprisonment. He knew he had no one to blame other than himself. It had been his plan to tempt Avery out of hiding and then pass him onto the McKenzies for the execution he richly deserved. He realised that the grief endured by Mary McKenzie had caused her to make the unbelievably bad decision to elongate Avery's sentence and he ought to have known better. Now he was responsible for releasing a wounded wild animal and he suspected innocent lives would be lost as a consequence. Yet despite all that, here he was trying to rectify an impossible situation. He had reached the conclusion that once satisfied Cameron was safe he would have no option but to come clean. And that terrified him.

By the time he had sorted a car hire the city had come to life and was waking up to a new and bright sunny day. He envied every single person he saw as made the journey away from the airport. This time yesterday he had been having breakfast in a quaint Parisian café and had laughed uncontrollably when Robin mimicked his useless attempts to order the food in French. At that time he would not have swapped places with anyone and now it felt like the world was ending.

He snapped himself out of his growing malaise long enough to call his deputy and extend his leave by a couple of days, before depressing the accelerator further down. By mid-morning he was on a familiar road that led to the McKenzie residence and he wondered what state Mary would be in. As if his thoughts had somehow triggered a telepathic reaction his phone rang and he heard her unexpectedly upbeat voice.

"How far are you away?" she asked.

"Literally ten minutes, what's happened?" replied Bare, knowing there must be a reason for her to call.

"He's dead, Seb, the police found him a short distance from the hospital. Superintendent Leighton just called to let me know."

Bare audibly exhaled and the pause was filled with Mary providing more detail.

"It looks like our man possibly injected before Avery attacked him, he only got so far away before the poison worked and he collapsed. I'm so sorry for allowing all this to happen."

"Are they sure it's him?" asked Bare, struggling to take on board the one hypothetical outcome he had not even considered.

"Yes, one hundred per cent. Leighton went to the scene himself before updating me. I think it's going to be okay."

Bare did not wish to deflate her but was far from convinced it was going to be okay. Police Scotland now had a double murder to investigate and if they discovered the true identity of victim number two he still saw the distinct possibility of his and Mary's entwined world being ripped apart. That said, his remaining hypothetical outcomes were now all substantially better without the presence of Paul Avery at their heart.

Mary started to tell him further detail about Leighton's plans to 'tidy up' the investigation but in truth Bare had stopped listening. He was now only a few minutes from her house and the dawning realisation that Cameron was now safe allowed him to regain some much-needed perspective. He brushed away a tear of relief that had appeared in the corner of his eye and with customary bravado cut the conversation short.

"I'll be there soon, we can talk then. Put the kettle on," he commanded.

"Fuck the kettle, young man. I'm pouring us both a generous single malt, I don't care what time of the morning it is," she replied.

CHAPTER 78

Avery stood in front of his still-tied captive and slowly clapped his hands in praise.

"That was awesome, I mean really well done. I literally could not have scripted that better," he enthused.

"You did script it," said Leighton wearily.

"Ah, but the additional little details and your demand to be released from the McKenzie stranglehold at the end just made it all so believable," laughed Avery.

"So what now?" asked Leighton with more than a little trepidation.

"Well, now you have two choices, my friend, and in the short time we have known each other I suspect you're not going to be thrilled about either but the second choice at least allows you to live, finish your thirty years and draw that well-deserved police pension," said Avery.

"And the first option?" asked Leighton.

"Would see the sudden end of our camaraderie as fellow Detective Superintendents. Shall we just focus on option two?" replied Avery.

"I would like to draw my pension and live a quiet life. What do you want?"

"Excellent. Well, in brief I will need your car, some reasonable expenses and maybe a nice bottle from your collection that I can keep for a special occasion. You can return to work and make sure there is never a suggestion that Paul Avery was ever resurrected in

Scotland. In return I will take pleasure in killing Mary McKenzie, thereby ensuring your professional reputation remains intact. I'm sure you can square this all of as a feud between rival crime groups. What do you say?" said Avery, pouring himself a generous red wine.

"And we never meet again, you never come back for anything else?" said Leighton.

"Provided the expenses are reasonable. I'm not sure if I have any assets left by now so I need enough to start again elsewhere," confided Avery.

"You can have my unlaundered pile. There is about 20K, it's hidden in the garage," said Leighton, offering up the smaller of his two emergency nest eggs.

It took Avery less than ten minutes to recover the bag after Leighton provided the exact hiding place and he was relieved to see the notes inside it were of an English denomination. He returned to the dining room, selected a bottle from the wine rack and placed it carefully on top of the bundled notes in the bag. He then approached Leighton with a large knife in his hand, causing the seated man to tense himself in nervous anticipation. To Leighton's relief the knife was merely used to cut the ties behind his back and for the first time in hours he was able to move his hands freely. As he started undoing the leg restraints Avery poured him a generous glass of wine and topped his own glass up at the same time. Leighton drank it greedily to quench the thirst that had been exacerbated by hours of anxiety.

"How will you kill Mary McKenzie?" he asked.

Avery sipped his wine and considered the question carefully.

"I think slowly, but not take the amount of time she was taking with me. Ideally I will make her watch me slit her grandson's throat first," said Avery, matter-of-factly. "Does that bother you?"

"Nothing bad that happens to that family bothers me," replied Leighton.

"Or I could poison her, like she tried to do to me. I still have a syringe full," mused Avery.

"Have you done that before?" asked Leighton.

"Funnily enough, no. I did prepare some once but never had the opportunity to use it. Tell me, do you know how the poison would have affected me?" asked Avery.

"I don't know exactly, it was supposed to induce some sort of fatal cardiac arrest. The plan was to nobble someone in the pathology department afterwards so your death wouldn't even appear suspicious," said Leighton.

"Ah, clever, so the lack of police attendance at my bedside wouldn't have even been an issue. You have the makings of a promising serial killer," laughed Avery.

Leighton didn't hear the observation as he was too distracted by the sudden wave of pain radiating from his chest. He was finding it increasingly difficult to breathe and looked up at Avery with one last hope of assistance. No help arrived as Avery casually finished his own untampered glass of wine and watched the man's last few futile breaths. Once satisfied that Leighton was dead he retrieved the car keys and the burner phone that was used to communicate with Mary McKenzie. As he quietly left the house he hoped that the address Leighton had provided for Mary McKenzie was accurate.

"I really don't like dirty cops," was his final comment to the dead body as he left.

CHAPTER 79

Bare felt awkward at the duration of her embrace that followed his normal greeting, more so as they were joined by Cameron from another room. When she pulled away the smudged mascara around her eyes betrayed the fact that tears had fallen at the point of his arrival. Their conversation was initially stilted due to the boy's presence but after he had demonstrated his latest repertoire of dog training skills, Cameron returned to his half-played game on the console in his bedroom.

Mary rebuked Bare for gifting the equipment that occupied so much of her grandson's time but on this occasion she was grateful for his absence. She wanted to explain herself to Bare and was clearly mortified that her actions had the unintended repercussions that had occurred. Bare listened patiently having reached the conclusion that he was in no position to judge her actions, having been so complicit himself. He knew that going forward, if he were to have any meaningful relationship with his son he needed to maintain a bond of trust with the matriarchal figure sat opposite him.

As the conversation gradually became less tense it was interrupted by the tone of a text message being received on a mobile phone. Bare noted that the noise had emanated from her handbag and not the phone on the coffee table that he recognised as being hers. She excused herself and retrieved the second phone, clearly anxious to read the communication. She made no pretence as to its origin and read out loud that Alastair Leighton was seeking an urgent meeting to update her about her still incarcerated relatives.

"He says he is coming here. I guess you wouldn't really want to meet him?"

"No, I don't think that would be particularly wise, do you?" said Bare. "I take it he doesn't know about me?"

"No, of course not, he's somebody we have had on the payroll for years. I trust him but not that much," she replied.

Bare felt saddened as the casual description of employing a corrupt cop evoked memories of his late friend Jim Morton. He wondered what tactics the McKenzies had used to recruit Leighton and whether the man knew he would never be free from their reach. Mary appeared to guess what he was thinking and offered a reassurance about the future.

"I am going to tell him this is the last time I will ever call upon him. I meant it when I said before that Cameron will never be exposed to that lifestyle."

Bare didn't need to call upon his years of interviewing experience to know she was telling the truth. The fierce determination to keep her grandson on the right path was written all over her face. He suspected that the boy was more likely to be susceptible to his own bad influence than he ever would from this woman's.

He wondered what plan Leighton could possibly come up with to get the McKenzies out of jail and decided he didn't really want to know. Going forward, he vowed to keep his head down and just concentrate on his own issues, starting with strengthening his relationship with his son.

"I'll keep the boy occupied by challenging him to a virtual Cup Final upstairs, leave you to hatch some miscarriage of justice with your tame policeman," said Bare, excusing himself from her company.

"Thank you, Seb. You know he talks about you all the time," she replied softly.

Bare thought about responding in kind but chose just to smile before making his way up the stairs. Cameron's bedroom door was open and he stood for a few moments just watching the boy who was totally engrossed in the loud and frenetic activity he was apparently controlling on the screen in front of him. The boy's devoted dog lay patiently at his side and every now and again one of Cameron's hands left the console to give his canine companion a short reassuring stroke. Bare struggled to recall a sight in his previous forty-nine years that warmed his heart as much as the one he was now witnessing.

CHAPTER 80

Mary McKenzie recognised Leighton's car as it swept into the drive and hoped that he had followed through with his earlier promises to tie up all the loose ends and bring an end to her nightmare. She didn't wait for the anticipated knock on the front door and opened it expecting to see him approaching the doorstep. Slightly perplexed that no one was there she took a couple of steps outside and used her hand to shield the sun as she tried to peer inside his parked car.

In an instant her hair was violently pulled backwards and she felt the unmistakable sharp cold steel of a knife at her exposed throat. Her first thoughts were that after all those years of pressurised servitude Leighton had finally snapped. When the man spoke, his voice barely above a whisper, she realised instantly that the reality of the situation was a thousand times worse.

"Hello, you stupid little bitch, bet you didn't believe in ghosts."

She recognised the voice immediately and was able to turn slightly as he struggled to maintain a hold with his damaged hand. Her mind was racing as she tried to work out what course of action would give her grandson the best chance of survival. Her natural instinct to shout a warning was suppressed as suddenly she felt herself being forced face down on the gravel drive. Her mouth was now covered by his bandaged hand and she felt a knee in the small of her back effectively pinning her down.

Her raised skirt allowed him easy access to his target area at the back of her knee. She felt searing pain as her peroneal nerve was cut by a single slash of the knife but the palm of his hand muffled her scream.

"Now you can't run away while I go and find your grandson," he said, leaning close to her ear.

Her eyes widened in terror at the implication of his words and she tried to bite down on the improvised gag across her mouth. The lengths of bandage wrapped around his hand made the task impossible and he seemed to delight at the fact that she was attempting to resist. This double kill would be one to savour and he wanted to remember each delicious detail.

***

The match had been a one-sided affair and after witnessing Cameron's celebrations Bare casually walked to the bedroom window and glanced outside. He presumed the car outside belonged to Leighton and realised the visitor must have arrived during the cacophony of the football tournament. He wondered how the discussions downstairs were going and realised that, in spite of himself, he was curious about the cop's plans after all. He was about to respond to Cameron's repeated requests for a replay when he noticed something else outside. At the very edge of his field of vision he could see something lying on the gravel drive, something black, shiny and totally incongruous. It took him a few moments to compute he was looking at a solitary high-heeled shoe.

Bare knew he had to get downstairs quickly but first he crouched in front of Cameron and placed a hand on each shoulder to ensure he had the boy's full attention.

"Cam, I need you to stay here with Tyrus. Do not go downstairs until I call you, do you understand?"

The boy looked at him and appeared totally calm.

"It's okay, I know what to do. Grandma said if anything happens I should go to her room, she told me where to hide."

Bare knew Mary's to be the adjacent room so ushered the boy and his companion there before returning to the top of the stairs. The stairwell was in two sections and he had no view of the hall area until he descended the first section and arrived at a small midway landing area. As he turned to walk down the final set of stairs he saw Avery standing astride Mary who appeared to be lying very still on the hall floor. Avery heard the creak of a stair above him and turned to face Bare and for a moment time froze.

The mutual shock of each other's presence was evident in both their expressions but it was Avery who spoke first.

"Sebastian, I should have guessed, here with your family. Mary, you should have told me you had company," he said whilst delivering a kick into her ribs as a form of rebuke.

The groan emitted at least gave Bare an indication she was still alive and instinctively he descended a few more stairs before jumping at Avery. The sudden and very unexpected attack caused Avery to take a step back and brace himself. Bare's weight and momentum, however, was too much to withstand and both men were propelled toward the still-open front door. As they wrestled on the floor Bare became aware for the first time that Avery was holding a knife and he realised his survival depended on preventing it being used on him. He used both his own hands to grab Avery's wrist in a determined effort to neutralise the threat. Despite his weakened state Avery, fuelled with hatred, was proving to be the stronger of the men and managed to break free from Bare's grip.

Bare sprang backwards in an effort to put distance between himself and the bladed weapon, allowing Avery to clamber to his feet. Both men were now outside by the front door and began circling each other like boxing heavyweights. Avery waved the knife slowly from side to side, slowly advancing, seeking an opportunity. In his peripheral vision Bare saw that Mary had somehow pulled herself into an upright position and was being supported by Cameron. He immediately adjusted his position so that he stood between them and Avery.

Then there was more shouting. Cameron's voice, followed by a blur of movement that coincided with both men coming together again. Whilst Bare's focus once more became the weapon in Avery's right hand he felt like he was being stabbed from behind. It took him a couple of seconds to understand that Tyrus had been commanded to attack and in response was indiscriminately biting both men. He was relieved to hear Cameron call the dog back but the temporary distraction had unbalanced him. He felt a heavy blow to his sternum, causing him to exhale loudly and fall backwards. In an instant Avery was astride him and the knife was held against his neck. He realised that both his arms were being pinned down by Avery's legs and knew in that instant he was going to die.

"I should have done this a long time ago," snarled Avery.

Bare closed his eyes in hopeless expectation but the sudden loud crack of a gun made him open them. Instantly Avery fell to one side and lay motionless on the ground. The bullet hole was so central in his forehead that it looked comically artificial. Bare scrambled to his feet and saw that Mary McKenzie was still pointing the handgun that Cameron had retrieved from her bedside cabinet. She allowed Bare to take it slowly from her now trembling hands whilst continuing to lean on her grandson for support.

"It was me that should have done it a long time ago," she said.

*

Within a couple of minutes a car arrived at speed down the long drive and Bare recognised the driver as being the nephew he had previously apprehended months earlier. Patrick McKenzie quickly alighted from the vehicle and walked past Avery's body without a second glance. It was apparent his only concern was for the welfare of his aunt. Bare realised that Cameron had followed an emergency drill and called the family for help whilst fetching the firearm for his grandmother. He sensed that the only thing that had not gone according to plan was the dog attack. It was probably his imagination but Tyrus, now sitting at Cameron's feet, seemed to avoid eye contact with Bare as though embarrassed about mistaking him for an assailant.

Despite her injury which clearly needed medical attention, Mary insisted on giving out a number of instructions that the others felt compelled to obey without hesitation. Bare's assigned task was to put Avery's body in the boot of Leighton's car. Leaving the McKenzies in a conspiratorial huddle, he struggled to drag the body across to the car. Upon opening the boot he saw that the only obstacle to move was a cloth bag. As he lifted it out of the car he looked inside and saw that it contained a large number of bundled bank notes. He placed the bag on the ground and wondered how Avery had become so wealthy so quickly. By the time he had struggled to lift the corpse into the boot he was joined at the car by Patrick McKenzie who held out his hand for the car keys Bare had retrieved from Avery's pocket.

"It's my job to get rid of the rubbish," Patrick said by way of explanation.

Bare shrugged and watched as the car drove away before rejoining Mary and Cameron.

"You might want to disappear too. I have a doctor coming about my leg," said Mary and he was amazed at her regained composure.

"How you going to explain that injury?" he asked.

"He's a family friend, it won't be an issue. I'll tell him it was a gardening accident, you know I'm prone to them," she replied.

"I'm guessing your tame Superintendent won't be in a position to help you anymore," said Bare.

"No, we will have to find another way to get the boys out of jail. I have a tame barrister too," she replied with a wink.

"So it might have been useful for me to know you had a gun," said Bare.

"Well, when you get to know me better, Sebastian, I will show you all the things I keep hidden in my bedside cabinet," she replied.

CHAPTER 81

Five Months And Eight Days Later

It had been a good day. The work had been interesting without being demanding and everyone in the office had seemed to be in a pleasant mood. He had enjoyed his lunch spent in the company of regulars at the Swan and only had one more working day left before the glorious luxury of a long weekend off. Best of all, nobody appeared to know within the work environment that today marked his birthday. Julia had always teased him about being a 'miserable sod' when it came to birthdays and had delighted in sending in balloons to publicly mark the occasion. But today he had only received a virtual version within a text message from Robin and that had suited him perfectly.

As he began contemplating an early finish to the working day he sensed something was afoot in the main office that was adjacent to his. Suddenly the appearance of numerous people at his door confirmed his worst fears. Emerging from the now singing group and carrying a cake complete with lit candles was Sharon Brady, her face illuminated with mischievous delight.

His forced smile fooled no one and perversely appeared to amplify their song even more before they took it in turns to provide their repetitive best wishes for the day. It took an age for them to patiently wait for their slice of the iced sponge cake and to depart to the main office. Finally it was just him, Sharon and a severely depleted, lovingly made, home-baked tribute to making it to a half century.

"Thanks," he said and his forced gratitude made her laugh and nearly choke as she tasted her own creation.

"Don't be so grumpy. You didn't think I'd forget, did you?"

Bare didn't answer as he took a first taste of a cake so delicious he almost forgave her there and then.

"And I'm guessing you have no plans tonight, so you are coming to ours for dinner," she added.

"Oh, it's officially 'ours' now, is it? Does Gareth know you have formally taken over his bachelor pad?" teased Bare.

"Yep, I've moved all my stuff in by stealth over the last few weeks so it's officially our house now," laughed Brady.

"I am happy for you. He's a lucky guy, Sharon. I give it six weeks," said Bare, causing Brady to immediately throw the remains of her plate at him in a playful response.

After a half-hearted protestation Bare happily agreed to attend the Jones-Brady residence at 7pm that evening, figuring he would spend the intervening time back at the Swan for a pre-dinner drink. Knowing it would be unwise to take his car based on his intended alcohol intake, Bare left the police station via the pedestrian public exit. Just as he reached the door he was called back by the station clerk working the early evening shift.

"Happy birthday, sir," said Beryl, who had seen him progress through the ranks over the years. She handed him a gift-wrapped rectangular box.

"Thanks, Beryl. You shouldn't have," he said, accepting the gift with genuine surprise.

"I didn't, it arrived earlier," she replied flatly.

Slightly embarrassed, Bare accepted the gift and hurriedly left the building. As he walked down the street he saw a card was affixed to the box and curiosity made him stop and open it. He smiled as saw the card depicted a Scotsman lifting his kilt to reveal a Happy Birthday message underneath.

As he walked further toward the pub his phone indicated a new message and he was pleased to see it was from Cameron wishing him a happy birthday. Rather than return a text message he called the number and it was answered almost immediately by his son.

"Hello, mate, thanks for the text. What you up to?" said Bare.

"Playing FIFA. Happy birthday," replied Cameron whilst concentrating heavily on the virtual on-screen match that was approaching a critical point.

"Predictable. Well, thank your grandmother for the gift and I'll see you at the weekend, okay?" said Bare, realising any longer conversation would not compete with the computer game.

"Okay, Dad. Laters," said Cameron.

The sound of Cameron so freely using that term was still a wonderful novelty for Bare and he smiled broadly as he replaced the phone in his pocket.

As Cameron skilfully used the control console with a flurry of finger activity his grandmother limped into his room, still not totally recovered from her injury.

"Was that your dad on the phone?" she asked.

"Yes, and he said thank you for his present," replied Cameron without averting his eyes from the screen.

Mary McKenzie looked across at the gift-wrapped package on the table awaiting Bare's arrival at the weekend and shrugged her shoulders before leaving the room.

At 7.30pm Bare arrived for his dinner celebration with apologies for his timekeeping. The lipstick on his face and collar suggested that Rona had also been aware it was his birthday and had congratulated him in front of cheering patrons at the Swan.

"Happy birthday, mate," said Gareth, shaking his hand with genuine affection.

"Thanks, I've brought a bottle," said Bare handing him the

opened gift.

"Blimey, someone likes you. This is much more decent than the stuff you normally drink," said Jones, examining the label with knowledgeable scrutiny.

"Yes, I've been very lucky this year," replied Bare.

The three friends sat at the dining table and Sharon brought out the plates of food. The meal had been perfectly prepared even to the extent that she had anticipated he would be late. Gareth Jones filled his glass and that of Bare's but gave Sharon some sparkling water.

Bare immediately saw the knowing look the pair exchanged and didn't need to question her choice not to drink alcohol. He smiled at the knowledge that they were both experiencing the new feeling of being a parent and they all raised their glasses.

"To new beginnings," said Bare.

EPILOGUE

Five Months And Eight Days Earlier

The chime above the door signalled the arrival of a new customer. Mrs Storey looked up from her position seated behind the counter expecting to see a familiar face. The Post Office tended to be used by a diminishing number of nearby residents these days, so she was surprised to see a stranger. Something about the man's demeanour and appearance made her feel uneasy so she covertly pressed a button that was used to summon the assistance of her husband.

Although the man was dressed smartly it appeared to be a poorly fitted suit and she could not help but notice his heavily bandaged hand. As he approached the counter she was relieved to see her husband emerge from a side door and greet the stranger himself. Unexpectedly the man spoke in a refined accent and she felt that her initial perception of him may have been ill-judged.

"I was wondering if you could help me?" enquired Avery.

"We will try our best," responded Mrs Storey and her interjection told her husband his requested presence was no longer necessary.

Avery smiled and produced a bottle of wine from the bag he was holding with his uninjured hand.

"I want to send this as a gift to a friend but his birthday is not for a few months, so would it be possible to delay its dispatch?" he asked.

The Storeys looked at each other before the husband asked the obvious question.

"Why don't you just send it nearer the time?"

"I am afraid I have been going through a difficult time. I had a recent episode at the hospital where it was touch and go. I just want to ensure he gets it if something were to happen to me in the interim," explained Avery.

"Oh, you poor man. Yes, of course we can do that for you, just let us have the details. I can package it up for you if that helps?" said a positively gushing Mrs Storey, now mortified at her insensitivity.

"Oh, that's so kind of you. Could you include a card for me too?" asked Avery, having seen a small number on display nearby.

"Yes, of course, choose the one you want," she replied.

Avery selected a comic one depicting a man in a kilt and placed it on the counter. He saw that Mr Storey was inspecting the bottle of wine and hoped his efforts to conceal the syringe site in the cork had worked.

"That's an exceptional bottle, if I might say so. Is your friend a connoisseur?" asked Mr Storey who was clearly impressed.

"No, not at all, he is just someone I am lucky to have in my life. I doubt he will even know what it is," laughed Avery.

After a few more pleasantries were exchanged, Avery departed en route to the McKenzie residence. He hoped that after killing Mary he would get an opportunity to visit Bare long before his birthday present ever arrived, but it was always good to have a backup plan.

"He seemed like a nice man," said Mrs Storey.

"Aye, considering you obviously thought he was here to rob the place. I don't know why we are putting ourselves out for him, sounds like a weird request to me," replied her husband.

"Because it's good to do nice things for nice people. Not that you would know anything about that," she replied pointedly.

Mr Storey ignored the thinly veiled reference to his past misdemeanours and was grateful that his wife had never fully discovered the extent of his behaviour. Instead he concentrated on the wine bottle label which reaffirmed his jealous appreciation of its vintage.

"You had better put a note in the diary so we don't forget to send his mate his present," he added.

"Yes, it's done already, now you package it up and I'll go make us some tea," she said, causing him to wearily accept the task.

They had been married thirty-five years and it annoyed him that she delegated menial tasks to him with increased regularity. He felt that he was due some fortune.

After she had gone he studied the bottle again, feeling resentful that it was going to be wasted on someone who would apparently not appreciate its worth. After checking his wife was out of sight he selected a bottle he had for sale in the shop half of the premises. The labels were quite similar but the values were vastly different. He placed the inferior bottle into the box due to be posted and hid the original away for later transfer to his private collection. He smiled as he remembered a previous lecture from his wife about so called 'karma' and made a two fingered gesture to the kitchen doorway.

"You'll never know what you missed, Mr Bare, but rest assured I will raise a glass and toast you on your birthday," he muttered to himself.

THE END

Printed in Great Britain
by Amazon